TABLE ROCK

TABLE ROCK

Les Savage, Jr.

Walker and Company
New York

First published in the United States of America in 1993 by Walker Publishing
Company, Inc.

Published simultaneously in Canada by Thomas Allen & Son Canada, Limited,
Markham, Ontario

Library of Congress Cataloging-in-Publication Data
Savage, Les.
Table rock / Les Savage, Jr.
p. cm.
ISBN 0-8027-1267-3
I. Title.
PS3569.A826T3   1993
813'.54—dc20   92-43526
CIP

Printed in the United States of America

2   4   6   8   10   9   7   5   3   1

FOREWORD

Elmer Kelton

LES SAVAGE, JR., pioneered today's introspective type of Western novel, and like so many pioneers, he suffered for his efforts to blaze new trails. *Table Rock* was the last novel he completed. It was considered so far off-trail that his agent, August Lenniger, had it rewritten by another author after Savage's death; it was published in a form completely different from the original draft. The *Table Rock* you hold in your hand is the one Les Savage wanted you to read, finally available as he wrote it more than thirty years ago.

It is against my principles to give away a plot, but as you read, consider how many ways Savage was ahead of his time, how often he departed from the formulary Western norm as it stood in the 1940s and 1950s. Again and again, editors were set off-balance by his innovations, and all too often they compelled him to compromise, or even to eliminate whatever challenged the status quo. They were nervous about reader reaction to anything that departed from the commercially established Western myth. The formula, the standard characters, had worked well for decades. If it wasn't broke, they reasoned, why fix it?

While Les Savage paid homage to the formula in some respects, he was constantly trying to fix it.

Take, for instance, the opening of *Table Rock*: a boy of seventeen is unable to bring himself to use a gun, even to kill for meat. In those days a lad of such tender age was almost never a Western hero except in juvenile fiction, and

Savage was hardly aiming at the juvenile market. Not until halfway through the novel does he provide a five-year passage of time so that the hero is a mature twenty-two for the climactic chapters.

As for the thought of having a hero unnerved by the feel of a gun, much less the sound of it, this was almost heresy in the traditional Western field. It is little wonder that agent Lenniger was skeptical of the commercial possibilities, given the tight mold into which the Western had been frozen.

Lenniger was my own literary agent for more than twenty-five years, and I can remember his admonishments when I wrote a story with a too-young hero. And when I wrote one entitled *Coward*, about a young man who had run away from fence cutters, he warned me that I might be undermining the niche I had carved for myself with Fanny Ellsworth, editor of *Ranch Romances*. To his surprise, no doubt, she accepted the story without comment, and it was later reused in a Western Writers of America short-story anthology.

It took bold writers like Les Savage to help break the hammerlock the tall, silent, self-confident hero and the black-hatted villain had on the Western of the time. In *Table Rock*, as in many other Savage stories, the principal character is anything but sure of himself. He is beset by doubts and given to introspection. The reader wonders if, when push comes to shove, the hero will actually muster the will to defend himself and those around him. Therein lies some of the suspense in a Savage story. That type of suspense is denied a reader when a hero can always be depended upon to "do the right thing" and never make a mistake. Savage gave us a vulnerable hero we could worry about.

In several earlier novels Savage broke the old taboo against the hero having a serious relationship with a non-white woman, though editors sometimes compelled him to soften the relationship and, in a case or two, eliminate it. In *Table Rock* the teenage hero builds a very serious relationship with the half-Indian daughter of a mountain man. Furthermore, he hints at a relationship between a white schoolmarm and a half-Chinese character, although this situation remains ambiguous. (One wonders if he might not have preferred the character to be full-blooded Chinese, had the conventions of the time been less restrictive.)

Nor does he flinch from introducing something of the exotic into his Western locale by giving *Table Rock* a Chinatown, with the authentic sights, sounds, and flavors of actual frontier Chinatowns. Seldom in Western fiction will you encounter such detailed accounts of Chinese living quarters.

Savage's mastery at characterization was matched by the intricacies of his plots. *Table Rock* has many unexpected twists and turns, as many red herrings to keep the reader guessing as a good mystery. Yet the plot is generally logical. After getting over the surprise, a reader can concede that each turn in the trail makes sense in the context of what has gone before. If I had to make any criticism of the *Table Rock* plot, it would be that one of the pivotal characters does not appear until well after the halfway point, and his involvement seems not completely satisfactory. But that is a minor consideration in terms of the total package.

Savage became a master of terse but colorful imagery, weaving it seamlessly into the flow of the story line. The reader quickly grasps the look of the characters, the mountains, the forests, the hidden cabin, the freight wagons and all the other physical elements, yet without descriptions impeding the forward movement of the plot.

I have always been grateful that I came along in time for a few years of seasoning in the waning days of the pulp magazines, for they taught a discipline I do not find matched anywhere today. Even at their most formulary, they required that a story keep moving. Les Savage was able to build upon his apprenticeship in the pulps when he moved into full-length novels.

That he died at age thirty-five was a tragedy not only in personal terms but in the fact that it cut short a writing career that was breaking new ground, pushing aside old barriers. We can only wonder what fine works he might have given us had he been granted another twenty or thirty years.

Even so, he helped prepare the way for today's Western writers who enjoy many literary and artistic freedoms he was denied. For that, we should all be grateful.

EDITOR'S NOTE

THIS WAS THE last novel to be completed by Les Savage, Jr. He submitted it to his agent in December 1957. Five months later he was dead. His agent felt the story too "off-trail" for editors and the reading public, and so, after the author's death, the agent turned an outline of the novel over to another of his clients, who drafted a different version, published under the title *Gun Shy*, by Les Savage, Jr., and Dudley Dean.

Table Rock, as Les Savage, Jr., intended it, appears here in print for the first time.

CHAPTER 1

THERE WERE GUNSHOTS down in Table Rock, half a mile away, bringing Gordon Conners to his feet with as great a shock as if the gunfire had been near his ear. From his high vantage on the hill, he stared down at the houses flung like toy blocks beneath the immense, flat-topped rock that gave the town its name. Cattle had brought its recent boom, and its trouble. There was already a war between the big beef operators and the nesters, and more rustling than the few lawmen of the district could handle. The shots could have meant anything.

His startled breathing fluttered in his bony chest, which was more undeveloped than that of most boys of seventeen. Within moments Opal Hamilton came through the cottonwoods, riding her black mare sidesaddle. She was the schoolteacher for Table Rock. Only twenty years old, she regarded her students with a deep concern that showed a maturity beyond her years.

"Do you always come up here when you want to be alone, Gordon?" she asked, surprised to see him.

He shrugged uncomfortably. "I guess so. What's going on in town?"

"More rustling trouble, I suppose." She bent out of the saddle to peer at his face. "The shots didn't frighten you, did they, Gordon?"

He wheeled from her impatiently. "Haven't we gone through this before, Miss Hamilton? I can hear a little better than most people, so I can't help jumping when a gun goes off."

"It doesn't actually hurt your ears?"

1

"No. The shock of it is close to pain, but you couldn't say it really hurts."

"Then it must do something else, to leave you in this state. Are you frightened by it, Gordon?"

"You asked me that before," he said angrily.

"You weren't in school again today," she murmured. "Was it because of Jack Halleck?"

"What's he got to do with it?"

"You almost had a fight with him in the yard yesterday. I saw it, Gordon. Are you afraid of him?"

He snapped his dark, shaggy head back to her. "Why do you keep repeating that? Does it matter so much whether I'm afraid or not?"

"I wouldn't want to think you were a coward, Gordon. You're the most sensitive boy I've ever known, but your sensitivity doesn't mean you need to be afraid of things. Sensitivity and refinement could very easily make a person of higher caliber than the average . . . with a courage of higher caliber."

She paused a moment. When he would not answer, she drew a heavy breath, saying, "I'll have to tell your father you weren't in school today, Gordon." She tried to seem stern as she said it even though she knew she could never do such a thing to him. It was just that she didn't understand Gordon and was unsure of her feelings toward him—and that frustrated her.

Mention of his father brought a small, strangled sound from Gordon. He could not speak the plea, but it was plain in his face, a face that revealed his subtlest, most furtive mood as faithfully as a mirror. She saw it, and a relenting sadness came into her own face. She had not spoken, however, when the sound of horses came from the Table Rock road down on the slope. There were many hoofbeats forming a sullen mutter that seemed to put the whole mountain to trembling.

Gordon remembered the shots then, and some dark

intuition ran through him. Without a word to her, he turned and broke into a run; it held the light, unstudied grace of a deer, carrying him with surprising swiftness out into the cottonwoods and toward the road.

When he reached the road he saw a thick, oppressive cloud of dust raised by a large number of riders who had already passed. There were some stragglers: A man on a roan passed, riding bareback, with a rifle across the horse's withers. Then a pair of boys. One was Jack Halleck, a big, knobby, redheaded kid. Halleck's teeth, already broken from fighting, showed in his wicked grin as he caught sight of Gordon. He hauled up his white plough horse viciously.

"I ain't got time to give you that lickin' now," he shouted. "Your dad rustled some Crazy Moon beef and they're going to put him in a California collar and string him up."

Laughing with the unique sadism of youth, Halleck kicked his mare and gave her free rein, plunging on down the road. For a moment, Gordon stood rigid as a statue, staring after the boy. Thoughts rushed through him in a sickening tide. The feelings among the cattlemen against the intensive rustling in the area had reached a desperate pitch; a pair of saddlebums had already been hanged down near Green River.

Heart thumping against his ribs, he whirled and ran back toward the trees to meet Opal Hamilton coming out. "Miss Hamilton," he cried, "you've got to let me use your horse. They're after my pa to string him up for some rustling he never did."

Comprehension froze the expression on her face, and she stepped off. He whipped out the latigo on her rigging, pulling the sidesaddle off, and swung astride the bare horse like an Indian. Opal watched him ride off, her face a mixture of anxiety and an indefinable sorrow over what had been said between them—or possibly what hadn't been said.

The road took Scalper Pass through this range of foothills into Harrison Basin beyond, and he could cut off two or three miles by heading straight across the ridge from here. It was a good enough horse, without any particular distinction, and he pushed it as hard as he could. He had never been able to kick or spur a horse before. But now, without even realizing it, he thumped a tattoo on its flanks that sent the beast laboring up the rocky slope past the pool and on over the ridge.

From here the basin spread out beneath, a long sweep of fallow land melting into the furrowed fields and square patches of wild hay that marked his father's holdings near the middle of the basin. He saw the first riders appearing at this end of Scalper Pass a mile to his right and pushed his animal into its final spurt, praying it wouldn't catch a hoof in a prairie dog hole.

He had to cross the coulee to reach the house. Plunging through the buckbrush at its bottom, he caught sight of the cattle farther down, held by a pair of riders. One of the men turned at the sound of him crashing through the brush and, with a shout, spurred his horse after Gordon. The boy put himself low across the withers of his mount, kicking it into another burst of speed, knowing he would leave a windbroken horse to Opal Hamilton if she ever got the animal back. He raced through the pattern of corrals and barns with the single rider behind him and the bigger bunch farther down the road beneath their swirling cloud of dust. He threw himself off at the door of the sod shack under the poplars, dodging in through the opening.

"Pa—Pa—"

Bob Conners emerged from a second doorway leading to the kitchen and bunkroom. "It's about time you showed up. I swear, Gordon, if you keep on shirking things like this, I'll turn you out."

"Oh, Pa," called Sarah Conners from within, "when are you going to accept the fact—"

"Pa," the boy broke in. "You've got to get out! They're

coming to string you up. . . . They say you rustled some Crazy Moon cattle. I saw the cows down in the coulee."

"Rustled?" The pallor that blanched Bob Conners's face so abruptly was filled with all the significance the word could hold in this country, rendered by the feeling it had caused this last year. It brought Sarah Conners to the door, a bent, work-worn woman, old before her time, with corded, veined hands and sunken eyes lifted momentarily from their habitual resignation by the light of fear. Then Bob Conners was grabbing for his rifle in the corner.

"Get your ma out the side door," he said. "They're just as liable to get the both of you as not. Remember what happened to that Carrington woman down on Miller Bench."

"Out?" said Sarah, drawing up against the shaggy cottonwood pole framing the door. "I'm going to stand by you."

"You can't, you hear me?" shouted Bob, wheeling to grab her arm. "You get out the back with the boy. If I went too, they'd follow and get us all. Come on, now, Ma, you can get to Roland. He's in at his cousin's—"

"Bob Conners?" shouted outside someone.

It stopped all sound within the house, all movement. Slowly, jerkily, Gordon's father dropped his hand from his wife's arm and turned to face the door. The rectangle was filled with a dim sense of milling, rearing horses, back from the house, obscured by their own dust.

"Come on out, Bob," called the same deep voice. "We'll give you a minute. If you ain't out by then, we'll fill your shack with lead."

"Don't go," Sarah pleaded. "Wait for Sheriff Simms—"

"You know the sheriff won't be here, the way they're running things," said Bob Conners solemnly.

He drew himself up, licking his lips. "Listen to me, now. They ain't going to get this gun from me. I might as well die of a shootin' as a hangin', and the fuss might give you a chance to get out the side door."

"I'm going with you, Pa—" Sarah began.

"Get her, son," said Bob Conners. "Ain't no use in all of us dyin', less we have to. I'll meet you in hell with a horsewhip 'less you do as I say, I swear."

"Minute's up, Conners," called the man from outside.

"I'm comin', MacLane," said Gordon's father, and walked out the door. Sarah started to follow him, but Gordon caught her.

"He's right, Ma," he whispered. "We can't do anything. They're just as like to hit you as not when they start shooting. Please, Ma—"

"Put down that gun, Conners," MacLane ordered.

The voice stopped Sarah's struggling. She straightened against her boy, a strained look entering her face. She stared wide-eyed out the door.

"I'll keep my gun, MacLane. What is it you want?"

"You know what it is. We found some Crazy Moon beef in your coulee. A couple of my riders held it while the third came back with the word. You've known a long time that Table Rock ain't satisfied with the way the law's handled this rustling. You and Roland Bayard put your necks in a California collar with that wet beef. Drop your gun, now, and tell your son to come out here."

"Seems to me you're a little small to play God, MacLane," Conners said. "Nothing on earth gives one man the right to take the law in his hands like this and—"

"It ain't one man, Conners. You can see the whole town is pretty well represented here. We're fed up with this thing, Conners, and if our duly appointed representatives can't stamp it out, we can. Now drop that gun or I'll make you drop it."

"Oh, no, Pa," moaned Sarah Conners, and surged away from Gordon. Until now, he had been immobile with the sheer terror of this. He swayed after her, still clutching her arm.

"I ain't dropping it, MacLane," Bob replied.

There was a violent stir of movement outside, then the first gunshot. Someone shouted, and more gunfire crashed. That was what did it to Gordon. The sound seemed to shatter his head. He felt his face contort and sanity leave him. His whole being trembled with the awful, overwhelming urge to escape the sound. He released his mother and lunged toward the kitchen door. He was halfway through it before a dim realization pierced his terrible desire for escape. He found himself turning back to her. She had run to the front door and stood there with her hand on the frame, her face twisted with terror. The guns were still racketing, with the wild whinneying of horses and the shouts of men forming a sporadic obligato.

Before he could reach her, Sarah jerked, staggering backward. Gordon heard the bullet strike the earthen wall at the rear of the room and knew it had gone clear through her. He caught her as she fell.

He saw his father out there, down on his knees, still holding the rifle. The back of his shirt was soaked with blood, and his body was swaying. The rifle went off, answered by another fusillade of shots. This time, Gordon lost control completely.

In a primitive impulse almost greater than fear, he turned and ran not even realizing he had his mother with him. Panting, gasping like a maddened animal, he tugged her through the kitchen as the shots roared behind him. If any riders had covered this side door, they were gone now, pulled around front by the fight.

Gordon never knew how he got her to the coulee. He might have carried her; he might have dragged her. He only knew that some coherent sensation returned to him when they had reached it. He saw that the bullet had hit her in the ribs somewhere, coming out behind below the heart. She lay beside him in the dirt, gasping feebly. He could still see the house, through the wild hay and the pack-pole corrals beyond. They were pulling something up on a rope thrown over the branch of one of the poplars in front of the sod house. It looked like a sack of meal. It was Gordon's father.

CHAPTER 2

IT WAS A big house of whipsawed lumber, with a long front porch of smooth, round stones cemented with grout and a tall hip roof to shed the Wyoming snows. The sultry, nostalgic peace of a summer evening shrouded the building, filled with the desultory chirp of crickets, the lonely yap of a coyote out in the Cheyenne Hills. The house was on the Table Rock road, a mile out of town, and belonged to Frederick Bannerman, a cousin of Roland Bayard's, Bob Conners's partner.

Bleeding all over from a rough passage through thorny brush, sucking in air as if each breath were his last, Gordon Conners dragged his mother up on the porch. He would never know how he reached the place. It had been animal flight, thoughtless, headlong, driven. He was still trembling from terror and the shock of all that gunfire. He tried to support his mother as he knocked against the door, and was leaning heavily against the portal when it was opened that he fell inward onto the man there. Fred Bannerman caught the both of them, calling back over his shoulder. "It's the Conners kid and his ma. Come and help me, Roland."

Bannerman and Bayard were both big men, and they relieved Conners of his mother gently, carrying her to the couch. Then Bannerman went to saddle up and ride for the doctor. Conners found himself in a big leather armchair, with Roland Bayard forcing whiskey down his throat. He coughed, sputtered. Bayard kept pressing him for what had happened.

"Pa," he sobbed. "Pa. Crazy Moon out there. I saw them in the coulee. He didn't do it. Pa, Pa . . ."

"Slow down, Gordon," said Bayard angrily. "Get a hold of yourself and tell me what happened. Speak up like a man!"

"Oh, Roland," murmured Mrs. Bannerman, coming over from where the women were tending Gordon's mother. "Don't get on the boy at a time like this. . . . Come on, now, Gordon, settle down. You're safe now. You've got to tell us who shot your mother."

He finally got it out. When he had finished, none of them spoke. Crouching by Conners, still stroking his shoulder, Mrs. Bannerman looked up wide-eyed at Roland Bayard. The man stood staring at the wall, a big figure, heavy through the shoulders, with jet black hair and keen, penetrating black eyes. His face might have been hewn by the winds and hardships of the country he had lived in for so long, his brows heavy and dominant, his jaw square with the aggression of the frontier. The sound of horses came from outside, and as he turned, light flickered across the plaid pattern of his woolen shirt. Then Doctor Seigal was in the room, with his pince-nez and carefully trimmed beard square as a spade.

He had them move Sarah into a bedroom. Gordon remained in the armchair, still trembling now and then. He kept squinting his eyes shut against the sight of his father swinging from the tree, but could not blot it out. He was aware that Bayard kept pacing back and forth across the room, as if trying to reach some decision, smashing one big fist into the palm of his other hand in a habitual gesture. Subdued sounds emitted from the other room: the soft closing of a door; a murmuring voice; the clank of glassware. Finally the doctor came out, a frown pinching his brow together. He looked at Conners, then Bayard.

"She might have a chance . . . if she wanted to live," he

said. "But she has no desire to. You'd better go in and see what you can do for her, Gordon."

Conners stared helplessly at them. Then he went into the darkened room, where the curtains had been drawn. His mother was a dim, restless form under the blankets. There was the vague smell of carbolic acid, the dull glitter of medical steel on a white cloth covering the side table. Conners crouched by the bedside.

"Ma," he murmured brokenly. "Ma, the doc says you're going to be all right now."

"I don't want to be all right . . . Where's Bob . . . where's my Bob?"

"You've got to stop thinking about that, Ma. It's just you and me now. I'll try to do better by you. I never was much good, was I."

Her head turned toward him , and he could barely see her eyes opening. She caught his hand, the strength of her grip surprising him, almost frightening him. "That's all right, son. It's something you can't help. It never galled me like it did your dad. Just because you don't want to farm or learn a trade in town doesn't mean you're no good. Your dad?" A look of pain crossed her face; blood bubbled from her mouth.

Seigal came running in. "All right, Gordon," he said. "You'd better go in the front room."

Again it was the waiting, with Bayard pacing back and forth, glancing now and then at the boy, a strange expression on his rough-hewn face. The grief, the fright, the exhaustion had all held Conners in a dull stupor up to now, but his perceptions began to regain their former acuteness. Sensory impressions had always come to him vividly, sharply filling his eyes, his ears, with a constantly changing pattern. The bright colors in Bayard's shirt. The flashing light of his eyes. The subdued sound of his feet across the hooked rug, changing to a sharper thud as his boots reached the bare puncheon floor. Then saddle

leather creaked outside, and Conners found himself turning toward the sound. The door opened and Bannerman
came in, a harried look on his face.

He ran a hand through rumpled, graying hair, "I sent
the doc on ahead and stayed in town to get some word of
the thing. Tom Union came in the Cowbell. He'd been with
MacLane, apparently, and was pretty jumpy. They done
it, all right, Roland, and they're looking for both you and
the boy now. You'd better leave here."

"I can't leave Ma," Conners said, coming to his feet.

"You won't have to, son," said Doctor Seigal from the
door of the bedroom. "She's just left you."

False dawn lit the eastern sky as Gordon Conners and
Roland Bayard departed the Bannerman corrals on horses
Bannerman had given them. Conners and Bayard meant
to hole up in one of Bannerman's line shacks in the Aspens
till the feeling died down, so they headed northward,
following the Harrison Basin road to the southern end of
Scalper Pass, turning into the hills on a dim line trail. On
the flank of the watershed, with dawn coming swiftly from
behind the continental divide, they saw a pair of riders
come around a turn in the road far below.

Bayard called a halt, hoping the lack of movement would
hide them, but the men below had already sighted them.
The riders stopped, held a hurried consultation. Then
one headed back toward town, and the other turned his
horse off the road and started climbing.

"He's going to hang on our tails till the rest come," said
Bayard. "We'd better split up. Here's something Bannerman gave me for you." He grunted as he bent down to
unsnap the flap of his saddlebags. From it, he pulled a
heavy blue-black gun and shoved it into Conners's hand.

The boy stared at the shiny, morbid, utterly foreign
weight. Then his whole body stirred, answering the impulse to throw it from him.

Bayard caught his hand, saying angrily, "Don't be a fool. You've got to learn how to use one of those things sooner or later, Gordon. You may even have to use it to eat on before you're through. Here's some shells too. We'll try to meet at that line shack in three days. You head north. I'll head west."

The boy stuffed the gun in his belt, watching Bayard wheel his animal and head off. Then he looked down at the rider, close enough now for Conners to see the Crazy Moon on the hip of his horse.

Conners turned his animal and reached the crest of the hill before looking back. The rider was not following Roland Bayard. He was following Gordon Conners.

The boy felt the tension of being hunted, of running. He rode Bannerman's horse, a buckskin with enough bottom to keep it going steadily and keep it ahead. More riders had joined the first one in the late afternoon, and Gordon hoped night would give him the chance to escape completely. He sighted the stage road to South Pass City ahead, in the dusk, and dropped off down a talus bank toward it, striking the brush of a stream. Before he was through, he heard the underbrush crashing behind him. He put his horse into a run.

The animal stumbled on something and went down; Conners rolled through some chokecherry, tearing himself on the thorns. As he lay still, he heard the buckskin scramble up and go crashing on through the brambles. In a moment, there was a greater crashing, and calling, and the riders passed by. When they were out of earshot, he rose and crossed the stream, climbing to another ridge that overlooked the stage road, a dim ribbon now in the gloom. On this ridge, he paralleled the road, knowing it would lead him to South Pass City.

Stumbling, exhausted, he reached the ghost town near dusk, winding his way in through grass-grown placer ditches and crumbling sluice boxes to one of the rotting cabins. When he pushed on the door, it fell in before him, striking the floor with a muffled crash that lifted dust into his face, choking and billowing.

He must have slept, because it was night when he regained consciousness. He had a miserable time trying to light a fire, and finally gave up. A wind filled with the chill of autumn swept down out of the Wind Rivers and he shivered for hours in the cabin, seated on the floor with his arms about his knees, before finding sleep again.

The next morning hunger gnawed at his belly like a trapped rat. He searched the town for something to eat, but found nothing. There were gophers tunneling the main street, and he kept flushing jackrabbits from the empty shacks. Finally he found himself back at the cabin he had slept in, his gun in hand. He stared at it.

He had never been able to use a gun, had never wanted to. All his father's efforts to interest him in hunting had failed. He could not bear to think of the pain it caused the animals. A jackrabbit bounded from a shack down the road, stopped to look at him. He stared at it, the gun growing colder and heavier in his hand by the moment.

He stuffed it back in his belt with a choked sound, and stumbled into the cabin, sitting down on the floor in abject despair.

He stayed there for two days, drinking the brackish water of Hermit Creek. Starvation finally forced him to use the gun, and on the third morning he stalked a jack. But at the last moment, as he leveled down on it, he squinted his eyes shut. The crash of the shot, the buck of the gun, caused him to drop the weapon.

Trembling, bringing a savage, intense concentration to bear to keep from turning and running, he opened his eyes. The jack was bounding away, unharmed.

He found he was crying when he went to pick up the gun; the sound of his own sobbing startled him. Was he that weak?

Desperation drove him to try again. He waited for an hour till another jack showed up. Again he could not help squinting his eyes shut. And again he missed. There was nothing he could do about it. Whether it was from fear of seeing the jack hit, or his fear of guns, he did not know. He used all his bullets up that way. When they were gone, he crawled down Hermit Creek on his hands and knees, hunting berries. He found some chokecherries and ate too many, and was bloated all night.

He slept in the cabin again; his head was toward the door. The sun woke him, shining into his eyes. He was still bloated, and belched as he rolled over. He blinked out into the street and saw a pair of Crazy Moon riders coming up the stage road from Table Rock.

He huddled back into the shack. There was no back doorway. He was trembling and sweating as they rode by. It seemed to take hours. They were talking in low tones and studying the buildings. When they were past, he took a chance and dodged out the front door, ducking around the corner of the shack. From here, stumbling, crawling, panting, he made his way up through the rotting sluice boxes and lacing of ditches to the hills behind, sagging down in some thistle to stare back at the town.

The riders must have found some of his sign on the main road, for they had separated, with their guns out, and were off their horses, searching the shacks. With a deep, guttural sound of desperation, Conners got to his feet once more and started climbing the hill. First he used the screen of brush, then timber, topping a crest at last and dropping into the next valley. Here he turned north-ward, all the time, wondering why they should be so intent on getting him. Did they come this far for a mere kid?

He was in the Wind Rivers, now. With evening, the wind cut like a knife. There was a somber, mordant threat of early snow in the air. He had more berries that night, but tried not to eat so many. He lost his way the next day and could not find water. He must have gone out of his head with hunger and thirst, for there was a long blank space. . . . When lucidity returned, it was snowing.

He stared around him at the sharp, climbing peaks, the soft pelt of snow against his cheeks, and a deep, chill fear filled his belly. He was lost. He was going to freeze to death. The knowledge reached him with unequivocal certainty.

He got up and started walking in some dim impulse to escape this. Then he began giggling weakly. He stopped this, realizing he was afraid no more. They said freezing to death was not too painful after a time. You just went to sleep. Well, he felt sleepy. Then he felt some warmth. He seemed to be rocking. Suddenly he realized there was someone's hand on his shoulder, shaking him.

"I supposed you'd be up here some'ers," said the voice. "Let's get up, son."

Conners opened his eyes to see a seamed, bearded face bending over his. Beyond the face was a horse. There was a Crazy Moon brand on its hip.

"Which one are you?" he asked. "I never seen you with MacLane before."

"I'm Blackhorn," the man said.

CHAPTER 3

THERE WAS A spare horse for Conners, another Crazy Moon animal, a Choppo with rawhide laces on the saddle. They rode into the stygian darkness of the timber and Blackhorn melted into a shadow behind him. When Conners started to speak, Blackhorn told him to shut up. Fear kept him alert for a time, but then dizzying hunger returned and he began to sway in the saddle. He must have passed out because there was another blank space. When he came to briefly, he found he was tied onto the horse. He blacked out again. His will to fight was gone.

Once he did come out of it completely, he found he was lying beneath a buffalo robe, musky-smelling with age and riddled by botfly holes. By the uncertain, wavering firelight, Conners could see a calico mule and three horses tethered to a line strung between two trees. Camp gear was strewn about—blanket rolls, other buffalo robes, an Army pack saddle, tinware, and a rifle in a fringed saddle boot. The fire flickered in a circle of stones. Beside it Blackhorn crouched, watching Conners.

It was the same, seamed face, hoary with a curly, matted beard, ruddy as the flames of the crackling fire. The squinted eyes were almost lost in the network of wrinkles surrounding them. The nose was sharp and hooked and questing, with a great high bridge that had been broken and knocked over to one side by some former blow. The hands, resting in the man's lap, were as weatherbeaten as his face, covered with comparatively fresh scars that looked like rope burns, and older scars that looked like something else.

17

He was dressed in the greasiest, filthiest rawhide shirt and leggins Conners had ever seen, with a pair of black-butted Navy Colts in homemade hide holsters hitched around to lay in his lap with the tips pointing downward and inward toward his knees. He chuckled, finally, a guttural, hoarse sound, the scrape of a rusty file across metal, and it revealed his yellow, rotting teeth.

"Booger," he said. "The boy's awake. And all he does is just lie there and stare. Ain't you never seen the likes of Blackhorn Campbell before, Gordon?"

Conners raised up. "Where's MacLane?"

"Down on the Crazy Moon, I surmise."

"This isn't the Crazy Moon?"

The man cackled. "This is Blackhorn's camp, farther into the Windy Rivers than any other man has ever been, white or red."

Conners stared at him. "You weren't with those men?"

Blackhorn must have understood what was in the boy's mind now, for he chuckled again, in that hoarse, abrasive way. "No, boy, I don't ride for the Crazy Moon. The horses you saw were theirs. Two of MacLane's men are going to have an awful long walk back to Table Rock and vicinity."

"If MacLane gets you, he'll string you up."

"Well, now." The man passed a horny hand across his mouth, raising his ruddy, tufted brows. "If every man I stole a horse from was to string me up, son, they'd need more rope than there is hemp."

"Who are you?"

"The greatest horse thief that ever lived."

"But you know my name."

Blackhorn waggled his head roguishly from side to side, then rose and stalked over to where Conners was sitting up, still beneath the buffalo robe. He lowered himself slowly. "I knew your daddy, Gordon. I was a government hunter for the Union Pacific when it was building the track from Nebraska to Utah. Your dad was a grader then. I'd hate to have to count the buffalo humps I stuffed down his crew. I heard when he took up partnerships in Harrison Basin with Roland Bayard. I also heard when he was strung up for cattle rustling, and they chased his son northward." Blackhorn was staring beyond Conners. "I sort of been looking for you to show up. Lucky I found you when I did."

"You say you heard. How? That was only a few days ago."

"I got connections," said Blackhorn. "The leaves git dry on the trail 'long about now and they rustle a lot."

Conners lay back, gazing at the old face, trying to decide whether he felt safe, at last, or not. Some sly twinkle in the man's eyes disturbed him. Blackhorn looked aside sharply. A girl had entered camp, carrying a bullhide pail of water. At first Conners thought she was an Indian. She carried the pail to the fire, set it down, then stood silently gazing at Conners. He felt suddenly embarrassed, being caught in bed by a girl. He threw the robe off and sat up. Blackhorn chuckled slyly.

"This is Willa, my daughter. Her ma was a Lakota."

She was cleaner than any half-breed Conners could remember. Her buckskin dress was white, paper-thin and like satin from innumerable washings on river stones. It clung to her, setting into relief the maturing curves of her young body. Her hair was not coarse, as was so common among Indian women, but seemed to glow with a rusty fire, falling onto her shoulders in loose, natural curls, which Conners attributed to Blackhorn. Her eyes were onyx. Her solemn gaze was lightened by a dimple in one cheek and there was a hint of a smile that reminded him of rollicking Indian babies he had seen. Somehow, when they grew up, they stopped laughing in front of white men.

"Don't stand there agapin'." Blackhorn snarled at the girl. "Git the boy something to eat." He turned to glare at

Conners. "Never git mixed up with a squaw, Gordon. Lazy, dirty, lying—you can't do nothing with 'em but cut off their hair and flog 'em every day."

The girl's hand crept to her hair. Blackhorn reached down, picked up a rock, and threw it at the girl. She danced aside to avoid it. With her eyes now downcast, she stooped quickly and dipped some soup from a simmering pot hanging on a gauch hook over the fire. She brought it to Conners in a wooden bowl, along with a slab of pemmican. Conners started to reach out but Blackhorn took it from her before he could.

"Now, go rub down the animals," he growled. "If I find any gall sores on your pony, you'll go without eating tomorrow."

Conners watched the girl move toward the horses. She was not frightened or resentful; rather, stoic, with that withdrawn look Conners had seen in so many squaws he had encountered along the tracks.

Blackhorn would not allow him to eat as much as he wanted, cutting the meat up small and giving it to him bite by bite, feeding him the soup from a tin dipper and breaking up the pemmican. Afterward, the warmth inside him made Conners drowsy. He tried to stay awake, but he could not.

When he woke again, he saw that the fire had died down. It made only a dim, red glow against Willa, sleeping now beneath a buffalo robe. Blackhorn was sitting with his back against a tree, snoring softly. Restless, Conners started to lift the cover and crawl from beneath the robe. There was no evident transition from sleeping to waking for Blackhorn. He merely came up on his feet and pulled his guns out, all in one motion that came so fast Conners had not actually followed it at all.

"Somebody around?" the old man whispered hoarsely, bent toward him with both guns cocked.

"Not that I know," said Conners, staring at the immense weapons. "I guess it was me you heard."

Blackhorn blinked suspiciously. "Don't ever do that again. Booger! I might shoot you."

"Are you always so jumpy?"

"You'd be jumpy too if you'd had them on your tracks for ten years."

"Them?"

Blackhorn peered at Conners. "I ain't the only one that's jumpy. What are you doin' all hunched up that way?"

Only then did Conners realize how he was huddled up, wound in the robe by the violence of Blackhorn's movements. He shifted forward, but his attention must have given him away, fixed on the guns. It was something he himself had not realized till this moment. Blackhorn glanced at the Navy in his right hand, then back at Conners.

"Oh," he said, softly, understandingly. "I surmise I heard about that too. Not like the other boys. Always running off by yourself. Don't like school. Don't even like to hunt. Do these things really scare you so much?"

Conners shook his head, still staring at the guns.

"I don't know how to explain it," he said. "I could always hear things farther away than Dad. Or than anybody, for that matter. It made them think that sound hurts my ears. But I don't think it's that."

The old man put his guns away and settled down again, a strange leer on his face. "I had a dog that was gun-shy, once. I always figgered it went back to the time some kids had him as a puppy and shot a Greener off a couple of dozen times, just to see him jump and howl." Conners was staring at him so intently that Blackhorn raised his eyes to meet the boy's, squinting one at him. "Anything like that ever happen to you?"

"Uncle Ian, before he went away," said Conners. "I guess I was about four. I guess I'd already begun jumping whenever a gun went off. He said he'd cure me. He took me in a room and emptied a whole carton of shells."

"Damn fool," muttered Blackhorn, staring into the dying fire. "Just made it worse, I surmise. I fell off a horse when I was a kid and busted my collarbone. I wouldn't go near one for years, and I'm still leery of nags."

Blackhorn raised his head. "What if you was in a spot where you had to use a gun or get killed? I'll bet you'd be able to, then. That Remington you had was empty. You'd eaten off of it."

"That's just it, I couldn't. It's more than the sound of the shots. I just can't stand to see an animal hit, jumping, squealing. It twists me up inside. Dad tried to take me hunting with him dozens of times. It was never any different. I couldn't use that Remington. When I pointed it at a jack and squeezed the trigger, I shut my eyes."

Blackhorn spat disgustedly into the glowing coals. "Booger! I never saw the like. Like a damn girl." He got up, leaned over, and picked up the old Joslyn-Tomes in its fringed saddle boot from where it rested against the tree. Seating himself again, he pulled the rifle out and began cleaning it thoughtfully. He snapped open the breech and raised his eyes to Conners. "I thought maybe you and I'd be saddlemates awhile. But I ain't bunking with no damn girlboy. We'll take you down to some town as soon as you're well. One girl in my camp is enough."

Conners looked over toward Willa. He wondered, then, how long she had been lying there awake, gazing at him.

CHAPTER 4

IT TOOK A couple of days for the boy to regain any strength. Blackhorn spent the time outside camp, mostly. Conners could hear him chopping wood, or the distant crash of his gun. He came in the first evening with a buck he had shot, and they had venison steaks. Blackhorn did not speak any more about guns. Then, the third morning, the old man went out and saddled up a horse, slinging the Joslyn-Tomes in its fringed saddle boot under one stirrup leather.

"When you finish making that pemmican," he said to Willa, "start picking up the camp. I want everything packed to move when I git back."

The girl watched Blackhorn as he rode off, her heavy-lidded eyes smoky and unreadable to Conners.

"He works you like a dog."

"Like a squaw you mean."

"Why don't you leave him?"

"He is my father."

It was said with finality, after which she crossed to a purple heap of chokecherries she had gathered the previous day. Conners watched her idly as she knelt, pulverizing the berries in a wooden bowl, a handful at a time. Her presence, alone in camp with him yesterday and today, did not make him feel uncomfortable the way he had always been with Opal Hamilton, or with any other girl. There was something shy about her, completely accepting, but there was too much strength in her, a core too inflexible, for her to be really submissive, to be touched ever—however Blackhorn might treat her. She was not outgoing in the way white girls he had known were, never coy or teasing; she did not joke or giggle, yet she had a sense of humor and would smile when something amused her, a smile that was akin to silent laughter. Conners's clothes were filthy, his face dirty, his shirt torn, his shaggy black hair matted with burrs. Opal, who was offended if a man cursed or someone belched, as Willa was not, would have let him know how she felt about him appearing as he was now, had she been here. Willa seemed indifferent to such things. He crossed over to her side and knelt down.

"I'll help."

She allowed him to continue mashing berries while she took some strips of sun-dried meat and pounded them into a powder, using a stone maul. Conners resumed speaking to her; it somehow seemed easy to talk to her.

"Blackhorn said your ma was an Indian."

"Lakota. She died when I was small."

"You've been living like this ever since? With Black-horn?"

She nodded and kept on pounding a meat strip.

"Is all that he says about himself true? Is he really the greatest horse thief in the world?"

"Among my people—my mother's people—it is counted a great coup when a boy steals his first horse from an enemy." She paused and looked into the wooden bowl. "When the berries are all paste, you must let them dry in the sun."

Once the paste was partially dry, Willa mixed it with the powdered meat and some melted fat, then shaped it into a cake that she put into the sun to dry. They had been silent for some time, but forming another cake, she spoke again.

"I do not like guns, either, or the sound they make. The sound they make frightens me too."

Conners looked down at his hands, bewildered. He did not want to talk about it. His family, the people of Table

Rock, had not understood it; he did not understand it himself. How could he explain it to Willa?

"My mother used to tell me stories about the past," she went on, unaware of his embarrassment, or pretending not to notice, "and one of them was about her father, Great Cloud. When he was a young man, he went off alone to fast and sit naked on a buffalo robe. Tall willow staffs were planted at each of the four points of the compass around the robe, and ten bunches of tobacco at the foot of each staff. There he sang the Fox Dreamer song." And Willa began to sing, in a small but beautiful voice, *"Te Ke ya inapa nun we. Sunge la waste toke—"* She stopped abruptly, then, after a moment, resumed speaking.

"He had refused to go on the hunt for buffalo and the People had called him an ugly name. But there, on that robe, naked, in the dead of winter, a boy not much older than you are, he had a vision and he understood. His courage would take another form. And that is what happened. He came back just as winter was fading. The People were camped on a river that was in flood, with chunks of ice floating in the rushing water. A child fell into the river. The People said anybody would be killed if he went into the river—it was so cold, no one could stay alive. And no one would go, none of the braves who had said Great Cloud was afraid of the buffalo when he had refused to go on the hunt would go, but Great Cloud went. He went into the cold river and he saved the child. Afterward, the People never said the ugly name again. He became Great Cloud. My mother said there are many ways of being brave."

Conners was frowning at her as he was listening, sensing something was behind her words that she was not saying. Was this her way of showing him sympathy? He was surprised at himself: he felt none of the shame he had known with his father or with others when his fear of guns was mentioned. Then he heard something else and he looked toward the edge of the camp.

"You have ears like a dog," Willa said, looking in the same direction. Several moments passed before Blackhorn rode out from the trees. He pulled up and sat in his saddle, scowling at them, fraying at his beard with knobby fingers.

"I thought I told you to have things packed," he said to Willa, his voice cracking the space between them. The old man dismounted and walked toward the girl, a bowlegged, rolling shuffle, his large body swaying from side to side like a tipsy bear. "Lying around camp, fat and sassy, spinning yarns, or worse, for all I know, wasting time while I go out and hunt and risk my scalp to make things snug and tight for you. It's about time you had a lesson, girl." As he said this, he pulled out his Bowie knife, close enough by now to grab Willa by the hair with his other hand, lifting her from her knees. "Well, Booger! I'm going to shave off your pelt. You'll look as skinned and pink as a new baby—"

"No!" Willa caught at her hair, struggling, trying to pull away from him. "No, father, please—"

It was probably the look in her face, but Conners, without thinking, jumped to his feet and lunged at Blackhorn, grabbing hold of the wrist holding the knife, twisting it back until Blackhorn howled, dropping the Bowie. Releasing his hold on Willa to free his other hand, the old man pulled one of his Navy Colts. Conners, certain Blackhorn would shoot, released his grip on the old man's wrist. He moved backward, pushing the girl behind him.

Blackhorn regarded Conners for a long moment, then, with an ugly note in his voice, rasped, "Afraid to shoot off a gun, but you act mighty big when you're not wearing one."

"You've no right to cut off her hair."

It was not until Blackhorn, after another long pause,

sheathed his Navy that Conners knew he wasn't going to shoot, and he could breathe easier.

"I ain't never cut Willa's hair off, and she knows it," he said then. "If you don't strike a little fear into a squaw now and again, she'll get as uppity as a big-city fancy white woman." Peering at Willa from where she stood behind Conners, the old man smiled suddenly. "Start breaking camp, girl." He turned away and lumbered toward his horse, which was still standing, although nervously shaking its mane, where he had left it. Blackhorn picked up the reins and walked the animal farther into camp.

The girl gathered the buffalo robes. Blackhorn began to carry camp gear over to where the calico mule was tethered. Conners concluded that the mule was as ornery as Blackhorn: as the old man lashed the gear on the mule's back with ropes, the mule would nip at Blackhorn at every opportunity. Conners understood why the old man's clothes had so many patches.

With the mule and one of the stolen horses carrying the camp gear, only two horses were left to ride, one for Blackhorn and one for Conners. After he mounted, Conners gestured to Willa to climb up behind him. Blackhorn responded quickly, slapping Conners's horse while chousing the other horse and mule on ahead. Conners looked back to see Willa following them on foot. When he tried to rein his horse in, Blackhorn edged close enough to grab the reins out of his hands, then riding on ahead, set the pace at a canter.

"Leave her be," Blackhorn growled back toward Conners. "She's got to have a lesson of some kind. She won't waste so much time at the next camp."

"It ain't right," Conners protested.

"She's my daughter, ain't she?" Blackhorn was glaring as he spoke, twisted around slightly in his saddle. "You butted yourself into my business once already today and you've still got your topknot. Don't try it a second time, sonny."

They rode forward through the vast, pristine silence of this little-known range, with glaciers that never melted glistening on the peaks above and the wind rising now and then to rear through the thick stands of pine like distant surf. They struck a dim game trail and followed it through timber so lush it was almost tropical, with yellow autumn ferns thriving beneath the tall firs, and mountain ash shimmering against a jade backdrop of pine.

Conners glanced back toward Willa and saw that the pace Blackhorn had set was faster than she could walk; she was having a hard time keeping up with them. Willa was trotting, her face grimed with sweat, her breath coming hard. The trail became rough and steep and the next time Conners looked back it was to see her stumble. He could also see that her moccasins had been torn, probably by rocks, and there were bloodstains around the bottoms. Conners suddenly dropped off his horse, then ran forward and grabbed the reins to his mount near the bit, jerking them back out of Blackhorn's hand. The old man drew his horse to a halt and turned savagely to face Conners.

"Git back on that horse."

"She's going to ride."

"I'm her father. I got the say if she walks or rides!"

"Not anymore, old man."

A grimace of rage deepened the seams on Blackhorn's face. Conners was certain the old man would pull a gun; then, it seemed that Blackhorn might swing down out of his saddle. He did neither; he did nothing at all. Conners waited a moment longer before he turned, leading his horse back to Willa. She had regained her feet and now gazed solemnly, silently, at Conners. Then she reached out for the reins, took them from his hand, mounting.

Conners swung up behind her, sitting as close as he could get to the cantle.

Blackhorn's face was still dark with blood and anger, as he waited some fifteen feet up the trail, his eyes squinted shut. Before they had closed the distance, the old man let out an obscene oath and whacked his horse so hard while reining it around that it squealed and bolted down the trail, the horse and pack mule stampeding ahead of him. Conners had taken the reins from Willa, keeping his right arm gently around her lithe body. He could feel her tremble and thought she was crying until he realized that instead she was giggling.

For what remained of the day Blackhorn said nothing. He continued to ride out ahead, and kept looking for something on the ground. Conners found himself watching, too; he could see tracks here and there. He knew those of the marten, the paws printed faithfully in pairs, each oblique to the other, like delicate embroidery in the snow. And the others, farther on, that some might take for a wolf but Conners knew for a wolverine, because of the larger straddle. But he could not think what Blackhorn was looking for.

As the day waned, Conners did not feel chilled, nor for that matter did Willa, whose supple, rounded body rode comfortably in his loose grasp, so that even while watching for tracks he was constantly aware of her physical nearness. When they made camp at dusk, halting in a high park near a creek with only patches of snow still on the ground, Conners dismounted and then helped Willa down. No sooner had her feet touched the hard, still partially frozen ground then she fell to her knees, her face drawn in mute pain. Blackhorn sat astraddle, watching her, as Willa gathered herself, rose, pulling away from Conners so that she could limp across to one of the packhorses.

"Willa!" the old man called sharply.

She turned suddenly as Blackhorn slid off his saddle, and remained standing where she was as he ambled over to the packhorse, undid a diamond hitch, and yanked free a buffalo robe that he threw onto the ground beside her.

"Sit down."

Willa lowered herself slowly onto the robe, curling her legs beneath her so as to spare her bloody feet, which Conners could now see were a mass of open cuts, the skin discolored and swollen. The old man jerked the bullhide bucket from the gear and tossed it over to Conners, who caught it and, without saying anything, went to the creek to get water. By the time he got back, Blackhorn had a fire started and was heating some lard in a frying pan. He told Conners to fetch the horn of gunpowder he had in his gear that he used for reloading cartridges. He poured some of the powder into the sizzling lard, mixing it all together with a short stick, then carried the pan over to Willa. He knelt before her, putting down the pan and loosening her tattered moccasins with a gentleness that surprised Conners. Dipping his neckerchief first in the pail, Blackhorn washed Willa's cut and swollen feet, then, with the mixture of lard and gunpowder, he began tenderly to rub them.

"Old mountain-man remedy," he said without looking at Conners, "that cures everything from gunshot wounds to green sickness."

Blackhorn cut a strip from the edge of a blanket and carefully bandaged her feet. Once he was finished, Willa tried to get up. Blackhorn told her to lie down again, stay off her feet; he would fix the victuals. Then he showed Conners what a timpsila root looked like and told him to gather them from around the edges of the park. They shucked the roots down to the white, turniplike meat, which Blackhorn threw into the pot with a cake of pemmican for stew. Squatting over the fire, the old man kept muttering under his breath while he filled the coffeepot and stirred the stew. Conners was not sure if he was talking to him or to himself.

"I'm an ornery old cuss, Booger. What makes me such an ornery old cuss?"

Conners glanced over at Willa, lying drowsily on the robe, her face aglow in the warmth from the fire. It really didn't make any sense. Conners remembered the same contradiction in his father—the work he had done, the punishment he had taken, the sacrifices he had made to support his family, and the times he would whip Conners for nothing at all, or go for a week without talking to his wife. Maybe something happened to a man who had stayed on a single trail for too long a time, the way his father had, the way Blackhorn obviously had. Would it happen to Gordon, now that he had had to run and keep running?

After eating, Blackhorn cleaned up, and they turned in. When Conners awoke the next morning, Willa was already up and about, heating water over the fire while Blackhorn was standing at the edge of the clearing, studying something on the aspens. They were tall trees, slim, pale, and smooth as human flesh, but Conners, as he approached, could see slashes on the chalky bark a foot above Blackhorn's head.

"Them corky black ones are old scars," the old man said as he ran his fingers over the marks. "These lower down are still wet to the sapwood. Chances are we jist missed running into him last night. Not a brown bear, either. When they're that high, it's got to be a grizzly."

"Pa said they do that to sharpen their claws," Conners said.

"Hogwash. They do it for a brag. A new bear comes into the area, the first thing he does is check the claw marks. If they're taller than his, you can wager he ain't going to claim the favorite bee tree or the local she-bear." He moved around the glade, studying other trees. "The way this place is marked up, it must be a regular meetinghouse. If there's an onion patch hereabouts, he'll be there, and we might fetch ourselves some bear steaks. It's getting too close to winter to wait any longer."

He crossed to the gear and pulled out the Joslyn-Tomes, then loaded it. He looked from Willa to Conners, and a sly twinkle stole into his eyes. Conners had seen that expression flicker across his face before, as if there were some devilment on his mind, but Conners could not be sure.

"Give me half an hour before breakfast," he said. "If I don't find an onion patch this side of the ridge, I'll come back."

He stalked off into the trees, silent and springy as a young animal. The horses were calmly grazing on some sparse brown grass, but the mule, ignoring the grass, was peeling bark from a cottonwood with its teeth. Conners joined Willa near the fire, staring at the somber stands of timber, the snow beyond. He had fallen into a deep, bitter mood. Somehow he did not want to leave this. Despite Blackhorn's first disgust, the old man had not evinced any further feeling, or shown any desire to talk about Gordon's fear of guns, despite their confrontations the previous day. Conners realized how free he felt, away from the usual ostracism he had known in Table Rock, how comfortable and at ease he now was, perhaps, for the first time in his life. He was still thinking this when Willa's voice stole in on him.

"Do you know about the buffalo?" she asked. "Have you ever seen a rogue bull?"

"You mean the kind that gets kicked out of the herd?"

"Yes. Sometimes it happens when they are bad. Sometimes it happens when they are old. They become mean and dangerous, maybe because they are lonely."

"I reckon as how," he said, and pulled at his jaw. "I should think you'd get lonely, too."

"Sometimes."

"You ain't never had . . . ," he became flustered. ". . . boys, I mean, you've never been close to one . . ."

She would not look at him then, her face turned toward the firelight, which enhanced its coppery glow, making her appear demure, virginal.

"Blackhorn says I am too young," she said quietly. "But I have fourteen summers. Sometimes I dream. I dream that a young man will come on a spotted pony. The People sing songs, you know. They sing songs when they go to war, or when they go on a hunt."

"And this young man, will he be singing a song?"

"Yes."

"A love song?"

Conners was surprised at himself after he'd said it. It wasn't the kind of thing he would ever have said easily before. He remembered how ashamed he felt when he was alone with Opal Hamilton. Willa had not looked up; her lips, full and vividly red, glistened.

"Willa," he said softly.

"That is what Blackhorn calls me," she said. "My name is really Wiwilla. In Lakota, it means Spirit of Spring."

Conners's palms were sticky with sweat and he rubbed them on his britches.

"This young man—Will he have to come on a spotted pony?"

She raised her head, and for an instant the shyness was gone from her eyes. A dimple deepened in one cheek and he thought she was about to smile, but before she could, the water boiled and she had to turn her attention to moving the pot off the flames. It allowed Conners to take his eyes away from her for the first time since she had spoken and it was then that he noticed the Joslyn-Tomes resting against Blackhorn's saddle. He could have sworn he had had it with him when he left.

"Blackhorn forgot his rifle," he said.

Willa looked at it. "Maybe you'd better take it to him," she suggested.

Conners started toward the rifle, then stopped. Willa was watching him. He felt a deep flush climb into his face. Before he could move, a shot up on the ridge echoed down the long aisles of timber, a hollow, shattering sound.

"That was close," Willa said, rising to her feet and looking off into the distance.

Conners scarcely heard her. Another shot came, this time closer, then a third. Something dry and cottony swelled in Conners's throat and he waited impatiently for the echoes to die. But they would not die; they seemed to grow louder, multiplying in the timber, making thunderclaps against the sounding boards of the mountains. He didn't know what to do. He started again toward the rifle. He stopped again. He started in another direction and saw Willa watching him. Then once more he stopped. There would be more shots. He *knew* there would be more shots. Then he heard a noise coming up in the timber. It sounded like shouting.

Blackhorn appeared in the trees, running hard. "Git me that rifle, boy," he yelled. "It's a grizzly and my smokepole's jammed. I got one shot in that's made him mad as hell. Git me that rifle!"

Conners could see the enraged bear behind Blackhorn, a huge, golden beast running in a heavy, lumbering, incredibly fast pace, hoary chest covered with blood that matted the curling saffron hair. His head was lowered and he made guttural, grunting sounds as he came, spreading a shower of brown pine needles up behind his clawing paws.

Conners wheeled and yanked the old Joslyn-Tomes from where it rested, kneeling while he fumbled in the saddlebags for a handful of .50/.70s. Then he pivoted back to run for Blackhorn. He had not taken one leap toward the old man when Blackhorn tripped and went down.

"Get up," shouted Conners, lunging toward him. "He's almost on you."

Willa made a broken sound, seized a blazing brand from the fire, and ran straight at the bear. She reached Blackhorn first, casting the brand at the oncoming bear. The beast roared and veered away from the fiery menace, but it did not stop.

Willa bent to grab her father, but Blackhorn lay in utter quiescence on his belly. The bear was closer to them than Conners was, and would reach them before the boy could. With this realization, all thought seemed to stop. The rest was reflex, coming so fast he had no time to think of what he was doing. His father had shown him the action of a gun enough times in his attempts to make the boy shoot. And Conners had watched Blackhorn snapping the breach on his rifle the other night.

He did it as automatically as if he had been shooting all his life, jamming the .50/.70 home and closing the breach. The stock felt smooth and oily against his chest, the steel cold on his hand. He swung the barrel around till that matted, bloody chest covered its tip, and squeezed the trigger. He even felt no surprise that his eyes did not squint shut.

The bear lurched in its run, without going down. Conners caught at the extractor with his left hand, then opened the breech, shoving another shell in.

Blackhorn was rolling over now, in a dazed way, Willa still tugging at him, with the bear but a few feet from them. Conners fired again, and again, and the grizzly went down on the third shot, one paw dropping across Blackhorn's foot. Willa stopped her struggling to stare at the shining, curved claws.

Conners walked slowly, dazedly, over to them. The conscious processes were beginning to function again. He gazed at the great beast, with its lathered mouth gaping open to reveal ravenous, yellowed teeth, its stinking golden coat blotched with viscid blood, more black than red. He suddenly turned and ran off into the grass, dropped to his knees, and retched.

After that, he sat there, staring at the ground. Finally he turned back to look at the bear again, hesitantly. The sickness did not come again. Perhaps a lot of it had been reaction to the terrible excitement of those moments before. He found himself, now, trying to analyze what he felt. He tried to find the horror he had felt, watching his father shoot a deer, or a jack, watching it leap upward, then fall flopping and squealing to the ground. He tried to find the keen, frightening nausea he had known whenever he thought of himself killing something like that. It would not come.

I've killed something, he kept telling himself, *I've killed something.* But it did not make it any more tangible to him. He could not really define what he felt now, unless, with the first excitement gone, it was indifference. He was merely staring at something that had been moving a moment before, and was not moving now. In a way, there was a great letdown to it. He felt almost disappointed at his own lack of emotion.

Blackhorn was sitting up, rubbing his head. He stared at the bear, then leered in that wise, sly way at Conners.

"You done a good job, for a boy that was afraid of guns."

"I didn't have time to think about it," said Conners.

"That's what I figgered. Looking at the bear make you sick?"

"Not now." Conners walked over once more to stare down at the beast.

"Purty close one, wasn't it?" asked Blackhorn.

Conners turned to face him, with something new forming in his mind. "Was it?"

Blackhorn's face lifted sharply. "Booger! I wouldn't want to add another foot onto it, or Willa and I'd both been bear meat."

"This was what you've been looking for since we started out, isn't it?" asked Conners. "Bear tracks. I thought maybe you'd been looking for man sign. You were really looking for bear tracks from the beginning. I guess you know a lot about bears. Just where do you shoot one to make him mad enough to chase you, without actually killing him?"

Blackhorn gazed up at him with his eyes squeezing ever more tightly together in a sly, diabolical expression. "Now . . . just what do you mean, boy?"

"I guess you know all about Willa, too. I guess you figgered just about what she'd do."

Blackhorn grinned admiringly at his daughter. "She's a good girl. I treat her ornery as hell sometimes, but she knows I love her."

"Love. What kind of love is that? You must be *loco*, she could've been killed—"

Blackhorn looked down at the Navy revolver still in his hand. His eyes were almost shut. "Could she?"

"Let's see your gun," said Conners. Blackhorn handed up the Navy. Conners checked the loads, pointed it skyward, squeezed the trigger. He jumped with the sound, but felt none of the shock he had known before. He lowered the gun, too wrapped up in the wonder of that, for a moment, to remember why he had shot the gun. Then, he jerked his head back to Blackhorn.

"That gun wasn't any more jammed up than you were knocked out," said the boy. Blackhorn continued to stare up at him, until he could contain himself no longer and began to chuckle in his hoarse, abrasive way. For a moment, Conners was flushed with anger. Then he could not help but answer the old man's laugh with one of his own, a shy, wild laugh that lit his face swiftly, momentarily, to disappear in an instant. Blackhorn rubbed his fingers across his mouth.

"You can't say it didn't work, can you?" he said drolly.

Conners didn't think he'd ever been so enraged. "You didn't have no right . . . taking such a chance with her—"

"Chance! What chance?" Blackhorn lowered his eyes to the Navy revolver still in its holster at his belt. "The girl wasn't in no danger. You was here, wasn't you?"

"But how could you know . . . ?"

"Know what? It was lucky I forgot the rifle. It learned you your lesson, didn't it? Think you'll ever be afraid of guns again? Think you'll ever be squeamish about hunting?"

"Just because I did it once—"

"If you did it once, you can do it again. You're started on the road, boy. You proved to yourself you could do it. You found it ain't as bad as you thought, shooting something. You found out it had to be done, sometimes. It may take a little time, but you'll be using a gun as natural as if it was your arm before you know it. And maybe next time"— Blackhorn ran a sly tongue across his upper lip— "it'll be a man."

Conners's eyes widened. "What!"

CHAPTER 5

THE REST OF the day was spent skinning the bear and preparing the meat. Conners helped Blackhorn with the butchering while Willa plied her talents dressing the pelt. The next day, they set out, moving northward through the Wind Rivers. Blackhorn proved extraordinarily solicitous to Willa's needs, even letting her ride behind him sometimes.

At the end of the third day, late in the afternoon, they reached their destination, a small cabin Blackhorn had built years ago and in which he and Willa wintered. Inside the dank odor of rancid bacon grease, rotting furs, and sour leather was compounded by ancient sweat and a dozen other indefinable scents. The floor was covered with bearskins and buffalo robes. The walls were immense, undressed pine logs, scabrous with peeling bark. Hanging on the walls were a motley array of Indian warbonnets, long rifles, and what looked like a string of scalps in one corner.

Winter soon set in with a howling blizzard that swept down out of the north to beat against the Wind Rivers for days, leaving the mountains frozen and white. Conners, Blackhorn, and Willa spent their time comfortably enough, taking turns cooking the bear meat while Willa continued her work on the pelt. Then, one evening, Blackhorn dug into the gear scattered around the room, and came up with the gun Roland Bayard had given Conners.

"You had it stuck in your belt when I found you," said Blackhorn, seating himself in a barrel chair. He spun the cylinder idly. "These Remingtons ain't bad irons. The added weight you got to carry around don't compensate enough for the larger slug. But you're going to be a bigger man than I am, and we got to take that into consideration."

Conners frowned at him. "What are you talking about?"

Blackhorn leered at him. "You ain't going to stop with the rifle?"

Conners understood now, and rose swiftly in vague irritation, and started pacing the room. Willa ignored them, concentrating on fixing the beadwork on an old hide garment as she sat near the fire.

"Don't tell me you've had that in mind from the first, too," Conners said. "You proved to me there are times a man has to kill. He needs to eat. But the only reason a man uses a six-gun is to shoot other men, and I'm not going in for that."

Blackhorn was silent so long that Conners turned to look at him. The old man was studying the boy with a strange, puckish look on his face. He shook his head.

"Don't you really know, Gordon?"

"Know what?"

"The position you're in."

"I don't understand you, Blackhorn."

The man leaned back, tilting his head up to peer at Conners down his wrinkled, sun-browned nose. He smeared a calloused palm across his mouth.

"I've taken it for granted all this time you've known about it. Didn't your father ever tell you?"

"Tell me what?" Conners said impatiently.

"You know your uncle is in jail?"

"Yes. For killing a paymaster in a holdup while he and Dad were grading on the Union Pacific."

"Is Ian Conners guilty?"

"I imagine, if he's in jail."

"Then your dad didn't tell you," said Blackhorn, seeming to sag in the chair, to shrink a little, as if reluctant to go on. Finally he shook his head irritably, like a bull ridding itself of flies. "That was back in '67 when the Union Pacific was just about to reach Cheyenne. I was hunting for the railroad, supplying meat for the crews. I'd fought beside your father in the war, and knew him from then. He and his brother were on one of the grading crews I supplied. I don't know how many thousand men were along that track, but you can imagine what a payroll the U.P. had each month. It came in from Omaha and was going to be distributed at Cheyenne. But with the tracks not yet reaching Cheyenne, it had to be taken off the train by a stage at Arapahoe Wells. Unfortunately, your uncle Ian had noticed it as a weak spot and had mentioned it more than once among the crews. There were about fifteen minutes there when the sealed doors of the paycar were open to load the money on the stage. Sometimes the military escort arrived a few minutes late, and that left only the paymaster, the stage driver, and his guard.

"It had begun to snow the night of the holdup. I was down in the hollow with the grading crews. Your uncle Ian had gone to get some more firewood. We heard shots up on the tracks, and we all started running that way with our guns, thinking it was Indians. It took us about ten minutes through the snow. Your dad and I were the first to reach the train. We saw the paymaster down, and somebody running off. We didn't know what had happened at that minute, and didn't try to give chase. By the time we found there'd been a holdup—with the paymaster dying, and the stage driver and his guard already dead—whoever did it was gone. Before the paymaster died, though, he said he'd emptied his six-gun into one of the bandits. By then the soldiers arrived and set up a search right off. They found your uncle in a drift with a bullet in his back. He had an empty gun in one hand, and a sack of money in the other."

Conners had seated himself on a pelt on the far side of the fireplace from Willa, who appeared to be listening even as her hands moved rapidly. He gazed at Blackhorn in a strange, luminous way. "It's funny how far apart Dad and I really were. I guess he felt the gulf between us even more than I did. He never told me the details of this. I knew he seemed pretty bitter about it whenever it came up, and wouldn't talk much."

"I surmise," said Blackhorn. "Ian recovered from his wound, and his story was that he had heard the shots from where he'd been gathering wood and had come up in time to see the holdup. He gave chase, firing at the men. Either they shot Ian, or one of the paymaster's bullets got him. He couldn't explain the bag of money in his hand. That, and the testimony of several graders about how he'd been talking before the holdup, convicted your uncle."

Conners studied Blackhorn with narrowed eyes. "You don't think he was guilty?"

The old man shrugged. "Your father thought Ian was innocent. He started out trying to trace the bandits down. He must have been on the right trail, because several times he was bushwhacked, and you remember when his hardware store was burned in Sheridan."

Slowly the boy rose, unable to sit still, this new idea gripping him. "You aren't saying . . . you don't mean . . . this last time . . ."

"You don't think he rustled them cows, do you?" said Blackhorn.

"No. That's what I couldn't understand. Dad wouldn't . . ." He trailed off again as he saw what that led to.

"Now you're in the light." Blackhorn snorted. "Somebody planted those Crazy Moon steers in your pasture, knowing how high the feeling was running about the rustlers, then turned the necktie party on your dad."

Conners paced about the room, unable to take it all in at once, shaking his head from side to side. The things that had happened all during his lifetime began to come back now: the mysterious, irrelevant little things his father had said or done that should have held such significance but had never tied together because his father had never taken Gordon into his confidence. Finally Conners turned to Blackhorn.

"You said someone had been on your tail for ten years. The same ones?"

"One. Ones. How do I know how many? I don't even know who they are. Whoever was running away from that holdup that night must have figgered that your dad and I saw him and recognized him. That's why they've been after me. With your dad, it was even worse. I tried to mind my business and forget the matter. After all, I was married to Willa's ma and I went for a spell to live with her people. Then, after she died, I had Willa to look after. I didn't want no part of it, but your dad kept on hunting, no matter where he was, or what he was working at to make a living; he kept on trying to uncover who really pulled that holdup, so he could free his brother. Maybe he'd found something good this last time. Maybe that was why they were so bent on getting him for good. Maybe he gave it to his son."

"No. He didn't! I didn't even know about it."

"Do they know that?" said Blackhorn. "Do you think they'd take a chance?"

Again Conners paced across the room. It was going through his mind now, the way it had at South Pass City when those Crazy Moon riders showed up. *Why should they be so intent on getting him? Why should they come that far just for a kid?* He turned back to Blackhorn.

"MacLane owns the Crazy Moon. Do you think it's him?"

"How do I know?" said Blackhorn. "I've been dodging it for ten years, and I still don't know. Now, would you like me to show you a few things about this gun?"

★ ★ ★

The winter days were long and empty of labor, after the wood had been gathered and chopped, and the meals cooked. Conners found himself practicing more and more with the gun, despite his initial reluctance. Again his natural talents lent him swift acquisition of the skills involved. His eye continued to amaze Blackhorn, and once his hand became accustomed to the weight of the heavy Remington, it was steady as stone. It took him an appallingly few days before he was putting as many rounds into a space the size of a playing card as Blackhorn was, at any distance. Then Blackhorn said he would teach him to draw. He gave Conners a worn old holster on a black belt and told him to walk off about ten paces and turn around. Then, he said, he was going for his gun, and he wanted the boy to do the same. He held both hands in the air.

"All right," he said, and dropped one for a gun. He stopped it with the fingers just curled around the black butt of his right-hand revolver. Blackhorn's mouth gaped as he stared at the Remington in Conners's hand, pointing at him.

"How did you do it?" he said finally.

"I just grabbed it and pulled it out," Conners told him.

The old man stared at him a moment longer. Then he began to chuckle. It broke into that hoarse, rusty laugh, and he walked over to the boy, shaking his head.

"I should have known," he said, studying the boy a moment. "I guess I'm beginning to understand you better. Your ears must be a little more sensitive to sound than an ordinary ear, to let you hear the way you do. And your eye has to be a little more sensitive to outside impressions, to let you see as far as you do. Your reactions are quicker than most folks'. It stands to reason you're just as sensitive inside. No wonder it made you sick to hurt something, and it scared you to hear a gun, after what your uncle Ian did. Do you realize what you got, Gordon?"

"How do you mean?"

"If you could learn to use it," said Blackhorn, "if you could cut out all those inside things, the things that hurt you . . . like how you felt when you saw somebody shoot a rabbit or a deer—You learned to accept that, you found it had to be done sometimes, and when you finally did it yourself, you found it wasn't so bad."

Conners stared beyond him, understanding in a dim way what the old man meant. As it became clearer to him, the possibilities filled him with a vaguely giddy wonder. If his physical attributes were a little beyond most men's—if he could see a little farther, hear a little better, move a little faster—and it had been his emotions holding him back . . .

There was something about it that frightened Conners. He turned to Blackhorn suddenly, unwilling to face it. "Why are you so interested that I learn to use a gun?"

"Your pa was a good friend of mine, Gordon. I can't just stand by and see them go after you too."

"I think it's more than that," said Conners. "You get that rheumatism bad later on in the winter, or during a wet spring?"

Blackhorn could not help dropping his eyes to his right hand, then lifted it, guiltily. He flexed the hand, shrugging. "Not bad. Just a little twinge now and then."

"Like you had last night when you was trying to pull your gun with it?"

Again that guilty flutter of eyes. "Now, Gordon—"

"Never mind," said Conners. "I saw you. When you thought I was asleep by the fire. Can't get it out quick when you're all crippled up with rheumatism, can you? Slows you down to creeping. If one of those men on your trail happened to hit you during a time like that, he'd have it all his way, wouldn't he?"

"No," Blackhorn said angrily. "It ain't that bad. Nobody can ever get Blackhorn—"

"Be nice to have a young saddlemate along who happened to have some talent with a gun. A man you could depend on to use it if you happened to be slowed down by that rheumatism."

Blackhorn pouted, moving his head from side to side, staring at the ground. "Well, what the hell. Mebbe I was hoping you'd sort of stick around. Man can't help getting old. Mebbe I am a little slower than I used to be. Wasn't exactly nothing wrong with it. I did pull you out of that snowbank. Sort of a horse trade. I'm sorry you feel this way about it. And then there's Willa. I'm all she's got right now." He turned abruptly, muttering. "You know you're welcome to cut your picket pin any time you want."

"How about shooting from the hip," Conners asked the old man's retreating back.

Blackhorn raised his head, turned around, eyes blank with surprise. Then, slowly, as he saw the smile on the boy's face and realized what it meant, that harsh chuckle began deep inside of him, way down in his little potbelly, reaching up through his skinny chest to the prominent, hairy Adam's apple and making it bob like a cork in choppy water, coming out his parted lips in a guttural roar of laughter. Then, in a moment, this ceased.

"From the hip, hell," he said. "I won't even teach you how to do that. If a man's an inch over five feet away from you, you hold that gun out at arm's length. And only a fool would let a man get any closer than that. If he does, you don't need no teaching to get him from the hip. If you can't hit him that close, you might as well not carry the gun. I ain't going to have no fancy gunman in my string, boy. If you're shooting from the hip, it means you're in a hurry, you're spooked. I've seen it happen more times than I care to remember. Man gets rushed and starts plugging from the hip and empties his gun without hitting anything but ground. The other one keeps his head and stands there like he was target shooting and knocks the first man over with one shot. I don't say you should do anything slow. But I have yet to see anybody who was really good with a gun shoot from the hip unless he really had to. . . ."

So Conners continued to fire from arm's length. He did not let his singular reflexes blind him to the necessity of practicing the draw. There was not much else to do during the bulk of the afternoons, and he and the old man spent hours, inside the cabin and out, working the kinks out of his style. In the mornings, sometimes, Conners would accompany the old man hunting meat, and having to kill to eat it no longer made him cringe. Sometimes, too, he would accompany Willa in the mornings as she checked on her rabbit snares. He grew to depend on her quiet ways and colorful tales, talking to her unabashedly about his own youth and what it had been like living at Table Rock. But, in the afternoons, it was the draw and target practice. Conners could not deny that it held a certain unique enjoyment for him, the enjoyment of developing any skill for which you had a talent. But it was still an abstract skill. Within him was a vague, insidious dread—a wonder—that if and when he met a man, and had to shoot, could he do it?

CHAPTER 6

WINTER WAS PASSING, and it was February, with the ice beginning to move in the glaciers above the cabin, groaning and creaking all day long like some chained giant trying to break free. The breakup in the lower rivers came with a crackling roar one night that woke Conners as he slept on the floor beneath the robe Willa had made from the bearskin and given to him. The snow melted on the slopes, and spiny, red currant began to poke through the talus. Cranes came whistling down from the high sky, and Blackhorn said it meant wet weather. His rheumatism corroborated the cranes by getting so bad he could hardly straighten up. Then the first hunting party of Tetons passed in the valley below, and Blackhorn rode down to talk with them. He came back with a pinched, seamed expression on his face, and Conners knew what it was before he spoke.

"Couple of men down at Fort Washakie asking around where Medicine Canyon was. Said they was looking for an old horse thief with a cabin up there. That's me, Gordon. I knew they'd hear about this shack sooner or later. It's time we leave."

"Don't you ever get tired of running?" asked Conners.

"No use asking for trouble," said Blackhorn, dragging out his sougan. "I've stood and fought more times than I care to remember. It don't stop them none. If I get one man, they send another after me. There's one I never could get, and he always seems to be there in the shootout. He's got a star stamped on his boot heels."

They had less to take from the cabin than they had

48

brought to it. Their clothes were few and their winter's food almost gone, and Conners had used up a lot of Blackhorn's ammunition hunting and practicing with his Remington. The mule carried a light load and Willa had a Crazy Moon horse to ride as they headed southward out of Medicine Canyon.

Spring filled the land with ripeness. The rich black mud of the bottoms steamed beneath the sun, and green serviceberries rattled against the horses' legs. The water in Medicine River had carried down all its ice and now ran swollen and yellow, streaked with chocolate muck, eating away at black cutbanks like a hungry child. The ford swept over the withers of their horses at places, and they were dripping wet to the waist by the time they were across. Willa pulled ahead of Conners at the shore and he could not take his eyes off the way her hide dress clung to the voluptuous curve of her hips, until she was partially obscured by foliage on the trail. After winding for an hour in the forest, they hit the wider, old Green River trail and followed this toward South Pass. The sun, which had been hidden behind a bank of clouds, came out and dappled the earth with shadows thrown by leafing cottonwoods. They were in this deeply shaded aisle when the first shot came.

Conners's horse reared up and began plunging, and he took a dive rather than be thrown by the frightened animal. Rolling through the mud and down into a grassed-over gully, he saw Blackhorn duck over the horn of his saddle and wheel his animal right at the trees, jabbing his big Mexican cartwheels into the animal. Willa, who was far more fleet than the old man, jumped her horse across the gully, crashing through a leafy barrier of bushes to disappear.

At the bottom of the gully, Conners realized how exposed he was to the slope on the side of the trail. The bank was steep and muddy, and he had to use both hands to claw his way up over it. His head was over the lip, though he was not yet out of the bank, when he saw it happen, through the foliage into which the old man had ridden. Blackhorn was in the timber there, swinging down off his wheeling, terrified horse. At the same moment, a man came plunging through the trees with a rifle, going in a tangent direction to Blackhorn. When he saw the old man, he tried to turn and bring the rifle to a firing position. It struck a tree, blocking it off, and the man did not waste the precious time it would take to free the gun and change his position. Dropping the awkward weapon, he went for his revolver. Blackhorn was free of his horse by this time, and going for his own holstered weapons. He got his hands on the butts, all right, then began to fumble. Conners realized Blackhorn would never get them free in time.

The other man must have sensed Conners behind him, for as he came up over the bank, the man wheeled toward him, gun out now, and began firing from the hip in a swift, hurried crash of sound. The first bullet kicked black mud up on Conners's legs. The second chipped white bark off a spruce. Before he fired again he was dropped by Conners's shot.

Conners stood still at the lip of the gully for an instant after the man fell. Then he realized how exposed he was to the slope across the trail and, with the possibility of a second man over there, slipped into the cover of the trees, only now lowering his Remington from where he had held it out in front of him. Blackhorn had only been able to pull his guns about halfway out; he let them slip back into his holsters, and began to rub his hands bitterly.

"Damn rheumatiz," he muttered. "Man ought to go jump off a cliff. He ain't good for anything else. Time was I could have had that kyesh full of holes before he said Cassawatamie . . ." He trailed off, seeing the look on Conners's face. Conners walked over to the body, staring down. Blackhorn moved over and took his arm, tugging at him. "Over here behind this tree, son. I think there's another one somewhere across the trail."

"He's dead, isn't he?" asked Conners, in a strange, empty voice.

"That's right, son," said Blackhorn. He watched the probing wonder growing in Conners's face, and smiled faintly. "Like the bear?"

Conners nodded. "Like the bear."

"You don't feel a thing. All the things you thought you'd feel ain't there."

"It happened so fast. I didn't have time to think."

"That's the way it usually is. And now you don't feel a thing. That's how it is in life, son. You stew and worry and fret over how bad you think something'll be, and it ain't like that at all when it finally happens. It's so different you'd hardly recognize it."

"I recognize *him*," said Conners. "That man's Tom Union. He was in the necktie party that hung dad."

"Does he work for the Crazy Moon?"

"Not at that time."

"Which leaves us nothing," said Blackhorn. "Except mebbe to smoke out the other one across the trail. You go south a few hundred yards and find a way over that won't expose you. I'll do the same the other way."

"What about Willa?" Conners asked in sudden alarm.

"She'll be all right," the old man assured him. "I saw her light a shuck when the shooting started. She's more Injun than white."

Conners looked down at Blackhorn's hands. "You all right?"

Blackhorn pulled out his gun laboriously and fitted his index finger in through the trigger guard with his free left hand. "I am now. Let's drag our navel."

The trail turned several hundred yards south of where the shooting had started, and here Conners got across out

of sight of that other stretch. On this side the country
began to slope upward into foothills. He crossed a low
ridge and followed the timber of its other side to where
the ridge itself overlooked the spot they had been bushwhacked in. He bellied up through chokecherry and buckbrush to the crest where he could see the trail below,
churned from the hooves of their plunging horses.

Bluegrass began waving off his left, below him. He got
his gun into position, pulling the hammer back. His breath
began to accelerate with the tension of waiting. For no
reason, he recalled the time Blackhorn had been chased
by the grizzly. It had all seemed deliberate then and
Blackhorn had acted as if it had been. But now, knowing
what he did about the old man's rheumatism, Conners
could not be so sure. Then a seamed, dirty, bearded old
face poked itself from the waving grass.

"Conners?" called Blackhorn, from down there. "Willa's
here. She saw him pull out, but we found the place he was
shooting from."

Conners rose and went down. It was a muddy bench,
with the hoofprints of a horse smeared into the muck.
Blackhorn pointed to bootprints, with a star in the heel
making its print in the black mud.

"Tom Union?" asked Conners.

"Hell no," snorted Blackhorn. "Booger! Don't you think
I took a look at Union's boots the first thing. They didn't
have no star. Union was over across the trail from the first.
This is the man that was shooting in the beginning."

Conners stared at the star print a long time. Then he
looked up, first at Willa who was standing slightly behind
Blackhorn, and once more at Blackhorn. "Well?" he asked
finally.

"Fort Washakie," said Blackhorn. "That's where we're
heading now. This changes everything. The two of us
together make too good a target. Better we split up, for
me, for you, and most of all for Willa here. You can get a

job on one of the wagon trains passing through there, heading East. It's time Willa and me saw some different country. Arizony mebbe."

Conners's first instinct was to protest, but Blackhorn would have none of it, stubbornly pulling in his head. They rounded up the horses and the calico mule, and before they set out, Blackhorn and Conners buried Union's body in a shallow grave.

They moved northward through the Wind Rivers. Blackhorn had become unusually solicitious of Willa, tending to her horse at camp, and the second morning out he let her sleep while he gathered water and wood for the fire. Blackhorn, when he spoke at all to Conners, avoided all further mention of the reason for going to Fort Washakie.

Conners was happy to let the subject rest, too. He had killed a man and that fact began to undermine the security that wintering with Blackhorn had brought him. One side of him could still hear the thunder of gunfire, and a raw, nagging fear began climbing inside when he thought about it. The other side that had begun to mature after killing the bear and at the cabin was becoming so faint as to be almost nonexistent.

When they emerged from the Wind Rivers, they came out onto endless sage flats. The sage was in bloom everywhere, feathery, gray with a green tint. The earth itself became a sandy clay, changing colors as they rode, bone white along the creek banks, but red as blood where there was iron in it.

They rode onto the Shoshone reservation and found a main road, passing wagonloads of Indians all heading in the same direction. Blackhorn said they were going to the fort for their beef issue, a trip that had replaced the spring hunt. Where the Little Wind River met the North Fork, they saw Fort Washakie. The log buildings seemed to loom on the horizon like a herd of buffalo on the move. There were a dozen buildings, the logs black with age, the adobe water-streaked and crumbling in places. The Indians had set up camps in the willow grove around the fort or out on the sage flats. Some of them had pole lodges covered with buffalo hides, but others had patched Sibley tents that had probably been discarded by the army. Their linchpin wagons, pulled by crow-bait horses, were tied together with rope or rawhide; half the women appeared to be blind, or pitted with pox, while the men huddled, shivering dismally around the campfires. Conners said he had never seen such a motley group of Indians.

"That's what happens when you tame an Indian," Blackhorn said, spitting in disgust. "Build them wood floors and they git consumption. Feed them white man's food and their teeth fall out. When I first seen the Shoshones twenty years ago, they were the proudest people that ever shot an arrow."

Conners looked over at Willa, but her face was without expression. Still, the thought occurred to him that were it not for the old man, this might be the way she would be living.

They stopped before a scabrous, peeling log building with a swaybacked sod roof. There was a long cottonwood hitch rail in front with half a dozen army horses tied to it and a few bareback Indian ponies. Blackhorn said they should leave their horses and the mule and go inside. He wanted to see the sutler about the wagon train and it was necessary to go through the saloon to get to the sutler's store in back.

The ceiling inside was so low a tall man had to watch out for his head. Smoke from the camphene lamps on the tables created an oily yellow haze. There was sawdust on the clay floor, trampled black and stinking of spilled whiskey, sweat, and stale cigar butts. The bar was a pair of puncheon planks held up at their ends by two barrels, behind which stood the barkeep, a bald, smiling man with a rusty, tin dipper in one hand and a loaded pool cue in the other. Across the front of his padded waistcoat hung an enormous gold chain, an American Horologe watch dangling at one end, a watchkey shaped in the form of a naked woman at the other.

"It's a bit house," Blackhorn told Conners. "Horace over there will give you a dipper of rotgut from the barrel for one bit, pour it from the bottle for two bits, or draw a charcoal line on the bottle and let you pour your own for four bits. It's pure forty-rod—drop a man to his knees exactly forty rods from where he took his drink. You and Willa stand here in the corner while I go find the sutler. I don't dare drag no filly through all them drunken soldiers."

Blackhorn pushed his way into the crowd and Conners's glance followed him across the room until he disappeared through a door in the back wall. There were some buckskinned trappers in the crowd and a handful of Swede farmers drinking solemnly at one of the deal tables. But most of the customers seemed to be soldiers from the fort. There was a big, blond-haired trooper at the bar who was making a lot of noise. He wore a black Jeff Davis hat with the brim looped up on the right side and the crossed sabers of the cavalry pinned to its front. His buff coat belt held up his trousers, in defiance of regulations, and his empty saber slings dangled against his leg. He must have been busted to the ranks recently because there was a light patch on his sleeve where his stripes had been. When he reached out for one of the marked bottles on the bar, Horace rapped him across the knuckles with the loaded cue.

"No more credit on the four-bit drinks, Conway," said the barkeep.

Conway cursed him, lurched away from the bar, and shambled through the crowd, the brass hardware on his saber slings clanking dully. He tried to borrow money from several enlisted men, but they all turned him down. By the time he neared Conners, his face was flushed with a sullen anger. When he was only a few feet away, his foggy gaze swung toward Willa. He stopped, blinked his eyes, then leered drunkenly. "Yer a new one. Tell yer pa I'll give him a jug of whiskey."

Her eyes smoldered. "My father is Blackhorn."

"Even talks like a human being," Conway said as he moved toward her, heavy on his feet. He reached and grabbed her arm. "C'mon. Where's yer tepee? I'll pay yer pa later."

"Leave her be, soldier," said Conners.

Conway ignored him. "Git yer own squaw, farmer. Ain't you heard? The yellowlegs git first pickin's."

Willa tried to break free and the trooper gave her arm a jerk that almost pulled her off her feet, then started to drag her toward the door. Conners grabbed the soldier's elbow, yanking hard. It tore his hand free of Willa and wheeled him back toward Conners.

Conway cursed and swung a punch. Conners ducked aside and Conway couldn't stop himself from lurching forward with the blow, falling heavily into the boy. Conners knew he would have to go all the way, now. He grabbed the Jeff Davis hat and pulled down so hard that the pinned-up brim tore loose from the crown, blinding Conway, who roared as he reached up with both hands to tear the hat from his eyes. It exposed his belly.

Conners put all his weight behind the blow, driving his fist deep, Conway doubling over. With the wind knocked out of him, the roar became a bellowing wheeze as the soldier staggered backward into a table. The table skidded away from him, but Conway grabbed the edge and kept himself from falling. He straightened up, sucking in air, his face pinched and sick looking. All sound in the room had ceased except for Conway, shaking his head now, still fighting for air and blinking at Conners. The drunken fog seemed to wash from the soldier's eyes, which were suddenly glittering prisms in the smoky yellow light. He made a soft sound and went for his Army Colt.

Conners pulled his gun. It came into his hand cold, heavy, aimed at the trooper. Conway's Army Colt was only halfway out of its stiff holster and he didn't try to pull it any higher. Conners could see the surprise in the man's eyes as he stood there, frozen, his hand clamped to his gun. The barkeep's voice came out of the yellow haze.

"Shoot, boy. It's your privilege."

A tremor ran through Conners. His draw had been an automatic reaction, as thoughtless as picking up the rifle to shoot the bear, but now he saw that he couldn't shoot. He saw Conway's lips moving, cursing him mutely. Conners wondered if the soldier was drunk enough to complete his draw anyway. If he stood there much longer, doing nothing, Conners knew his hand would begin to shake with the rest of his body, and the soldier would see that.

"Get out the door," he said to Willa who was behind him. "Get out now."

He heard the girl move and started backing after her. Conway finally straightened.

"Careful, Conway," said one of the soldiers standing nearby. "If he can draw like that, he can shoot like that, too."

Conners heard Willa open the door behind him. He backed out and she slammed it shut. He heard a roar of voices from inside, wheeled, and grabbed her arm. They ran in the direction of a dark grove of trees, stopping only when they were into the shadowed cover.

"Conners," Willa said softly. Her voice was shaking and she was standing close to him. "Conners—" He didn't know whether she did it or he did it, but she was there in his arms, her body trembling. She pressed her face into his chest, her voice muffled. "Conners—why did you do it?"

"That's a crazy question to ask," he said. "It was natural
. . . I mean, I didn't think . . . when he hurt you, when I
saw him do that—" He broke off. "I mean . . . I love you,
Willa. That 's why I did it. I love you—" He was shocked
to hear his voice saying the words. Maybe it was the feel of
her body against him, soft, warm, like nothing he'd ever
felt before, or the things that had been growing in him
these past days every time he looked at her, the hunger,
the yearning, the want that was now rising up in him that
he could contain no longer.

Willa only pressed herself more closely to Conners. "I
hoped," she said. "I mean I thought I saw . . . when you
looked at me, your eyes . . . was just the way my mother
said. A person doesn't have to decide, or think about it. It
just happens. I have known for a long time . . . I mean,
about my own feelings—"

Over Willa's shoulder, Conners saw a light appear in the
dark doorway of the sutler's store. She could feel him as
he changed, his body drawing back, and turned to look.
The shape of a man lumbered out.

"Conners?" It was Blackhorn's voice. "Willa? Where the
hell are you?"

Conners answered him quietly and the old man crossed
to the trees. "What happened in there?" he asked, his voice
a low rumble. "That damn soldier is cadging drinks from
everybody and blabbering how he's a-coming for you. I git
the idea he's afraid to show his face outside the door for
fear you'll shoot his lights out."

"Nothing," Conners said. "Just some drunken yellowlegs." He hadn't holstered his gun, but was holding onto it
yet, his arms still around Willa, although more loosely
than before. He lowered his arms and put away his gun.

"It don't matter," Blackhorn muttered. "We got better
cause to skin outa here than that. The sutler said there
was a man in here yesterday asking about us."

Conners's mouth went dry. "The one who got away?"

"Probably. The sutler just said he was a tall gent, but slender, narrow kind of, and he moved like a snake."

"Why here? I mean, how would he know?"

"He probably circled back to find out what happened to Tom Union, saw our tracks heading north, and rode right for the fort. Chances are you'll be gone before he shows up again. A wagon train leaves for Fort Lincoln tomorrow. The sutler says you kin git a job wrangling the stock."

Conners stood silently, his face stiff with the indecision that cut him like a keen blade. One side of him said he should face up to the man, to settle for that ambush, for that business at the dugout, for his pa and his ma. Because the man was MacLane's man and MacLane was a murderer . . . and that tarred him with the same brush. Yet—thinking of the gun he had drawn so smoothly in the bar put a chill through him. What if he met the man? Could he kill him?

Conners licked his lips. "If I go with the train, what about you?"

"Willa 'n' me? We'll go on a long trip. A very long trip, with as much country between us and this as we can put."

"You can't! I mean . . . I can't leave you, Blackhorn."

"I done my part, son. I brung you as far as I could an' kept my faith with your pa."

"It isn't that. Willa—"

"What about Willa?" Blackhorn's voice had a sharp edge.

"I mean . . . the way you treat her, like a dog, or worse. You ain't got no right—"

"Who ain't got the right? She's my daughter. She's a squaw."

"She's a human being. She's a woman. I won't let you take her—"

"You won't *what*?" It came out of the old man with a roar.

"Blackhorn! I didn't mean it that way. But, damn it, yes I did—" He looked imploringly at Willa, who was only a dim, willowy shape waiting silent in the darkness.

"Son, I think I know what's on your mind," Blackhorn said. "You been makin' calf's eyes at my girl too long. Listen here—"

"Shut up!" Conners flung the words at him. He had never spoken to anyone that way before, and he was surprised at his sudden brashness. Maybe hitting the soldier had changed him, done it, made him grow up. He turned again to Willa. "I never got the chance to ask you. There's got to be a parson around here somewhere. We could go to him tonight. Right now—"

Blackhorn made an explosive sound. "She ain't going to no parson with you. Why do you think I'd let her git hitched to a Jonah like you? What about the man asking questions about us? What about MacLane? And you'll have that hanging over your head the rest of your life. They're not going to let you rest, no more'n they have me, mebbe less."

"It isn't that bad. We can get away, move on west—"

"Not far enough. Never far enough. Never knowing where it'll come from, or when. Every time you walk out a door, in every town you hit, a gun could be waiting in an alley. Or an ambush on the trail like the one where you got Tom Union. I won't let you drag her into that."

"You're one to talk," Conners flared at him. "They've been after you longer than they have me. How come you think she'd be safer with you?"

"Because you're gunshy."

"And you've got rheumatism so bad you're all crippled up—"

"No one has asked me," Willa said, moving forward from the shadows. "You haven't asked me what I want." Blackhorn and Conners both paused to look at her. She came next to Conners, taking his arm. "I don't care who's after him. I love him, Blackhorn."

The old man gaped at her, then turned abruptly and began pacing, rubbing the back of his neck and mumbling to himself. Conners only caught part of it as Willa leaned closer to him and he put his arm around her.

"That's the way the hair turns . . . old bear . . . going blind, rheumatiz . . . cub's now going to run out on him . . . can't count on nobody nohow . . ." He stopped, glaring at his daughter. "You really mean it, girl? You'd hitch yourself up with him?"

"I mean it."

Blackhorn rubbed his hand over his mouth. He studied Conners, then scratching his beard, he spat. "Maybe you're just doing this to git away from me, Willa. Maybe . . . if I'd treated you better right along—"

"It wouldn't have made any difference," she said.

"Ain't there anything I can say?" he asked. She gazed at him silently, not answering. At last the old man's shoulders sagged and he let out a long, wheezing sigh. "I must be getting old. Few years ago I would have knocked Conners on the head and dragged you off kicking, Willa. Well, mebbe I learned something from the Indians after all. They know when to quit fighting. One man can't stop a buffalo stampede by his lonesome. Better to drift with the storm. I'll tell you what, son. There's a parson at the fort, but Indians aren't allowed in there. The sutler's store is as close as I dare bring Willa. Willa and me can wait here while you go and fetch that parson."

Conners could not believe the old man had given in so easily. "You mean . . . you're not—"

"You heard me, son. Jump now!" He grinned slyly. "Afore I change my mind."

Conners embraced Willa, then turned and hurried through the trees, where he was soon enveloped in the shadows. A pack of Indian dogs yapped at his heels as he quickly skirted the Shoshone camp. He could see the fort just beyond, a shapeless mass of buildings silhouetted in the darkness, lights blinking at windows. It was while he was crossing to the compound that he was assailed by haunting doubts. He had to be *loco*. He wasn't out of his teens. Back in Table Rock he was still a schoolboy. Willa was at least a couple of years younger than he was. No wonder Blackhorn had fought the notion. How would he support her? He didn't really know how to do anything. As a wrangler on the wagon train, he might get fifteen dollars a month, but he would be heading East, not West, and he could elude the men who were after him, the men who had killed his parents.

Maybe he ought to wait until he learned a trade, until he knew what it was he would do, where he should go. Yet, how long would that take? And he loved her, Wiwilla. He did. The feel of her in his arms danced back into his consciousness, making him giddy with yearning. They would find a way. His pa had married young, nineteen. That was a little older than seventeen but it still was young.

And what had happened? Conners remembered his mother, the suffering as they went from one place to another, always searching, never settling down. Conners had never known the reason why until Blackhorn had told him. The image of his father hanging from a poplar branch before the sod house came to Conners, and he knew the same threat hung over him. He couldn't go back to Table Rock and confront MacLane. He would be killed. And if not that, there was the man with the boot with a star imprinted in its heel who had ambushed them on the trail, who had been following Blackhorn for years and was now following him. The old man was right. How could he ask Wiwilla to share the sort of life he would have to live from here on, always on the run the way Blackhorn was? His thoughts halted abruptly as a voice came at him out of the night.

It was a fort sentry challenging him. Conners said he had come to fetch the parson.

"Hell," the sentry said, laughing, "there ain't no parson here. What use would we have for a parson?"

Conners tried to make out the man's face, but it was obscured by shadows. Then suddenly he understood. He should have been suspicious from the first when the old man seemed to give in so easily. He turned and ran back in the direction of the trees. Blackhorn and Wiwilla were not where he had left them. The grove was quiet, sinister, empty. He crossed at a run to the hitch rail in front of the sutler's store. All of Blackhorn's horses were gone, the calico mule, even the mount Conners had ridden.

He began to tremble. He stood there, the anger gripping him, then looked at the other horses tied to the hitch rail. He might steal one of them and go after them. But which way had they gone? It was too dark to trail them, and Conners knew he wasn't as good at tracking as Blackhorn was, or at finding the old man's sign, if he didn't want it to be found. Sickness and fury gripped him, a helplessness. If that soldier were to come out of the taproom now, he could shoot. He could shoot him now. He knew he could.

CHAPTER 7

CONNERS SLEPT THAT night in the tall grass that ran along the riverbank. He was stiff when he awoke, his muscles so cramped he could barely move. He knew he must keep out of sight. The man who had been with Tom Union might return. He wandered into the Indian encampment, speaking with a few of the Shoshones who knew English. He asked about Blackhorn. The old man was not unknown among them, but no one had any idea where he might have been headed when he pulled out the previous night.

Conners knew that there would be a wagon train leaving that morning, but he had resolved now that he would not be with it. It would only take him that much farther away from Wiwilla, and he was certain she had not gone with her father willingly.

By midday, he tried to find some work around the fort, but most of the settlers were homesteaders who were having a hardscrabble time keeping themselves fed. Finally, hunger drove him to the sutler's store, where he made a deal to chop a half cord of wood for a meal. In the back room of the store the sutler's wife gave him some hogside and white-pot—a mixture of milk, eggs, cornmeal, and molasses. He was on his third bowl when the sutler came in and said somebody was outside, asking for him.

Conners froze in his seat. "A big jasper riding a Crazy Moon horse?"

"No," the sutler replied laughing, knowing very well whom Conners meant. "A little girl riding a calico mule. She's so short you couldn't see her in a cornfield."

Conners found her standing out front near the hitch

rail, holding the reins of Blackhorn's mule and one of the Crazy Moon horses she must have led behind her. There was a dark bruise on her face, and her buckskin dress was torn. Conners knew at once what must have happened. He took her in his arms, holding her tightly, oblivious to the curious stares of the homesteaders and soldiers passing in and out of the taproom. Then he thought of the man who was looking for him. With one arm still around her, he took up the reins of the two animals and led them into a grove of willows.

"Blackhorn made me go," the girl murmured once they were in a shadowed glen among the trees. She was dusty and so exhausted from the long ride and her obvious ordeal that her lips trembled as she spoke. "After you started for the fort last night, he twisted my arm behind me, his hand over my mouth. I struggled, Conners, but he was too strong for me. I tried to fight him—"

"I know, I know," Conners told her gently. "I figured it must have been something like that. He's a sly old sidewinder."

"We didn't make camp until dawn, and when we did, he tied me up. There was a sharp rock nearby and I was able to fray the rope. He was still asleep . . ."

Conners turned, picked up the reins, and moved the animals even farther into the trees. Then, almost out of earshot of the fort and the surrounding encampments, he dropped the reins and held her even more closely than before. For a while he thought she was going to cry, she clung to him so, her face buried tightly against his chest. It made him feel more a man than he had ever felt before. He had kicked himself as a fool last night, letting Blackhorn trick him so easily. He had worried that he and Wiwilla were too young, but now any doubts he might have had were gone.

"We can't stay here," he said. "Blackhorn will track you back here."

"Not very fast," she said. "I stampeded the other horses when I left."

He pulled her back, looking down into the dark pools of her brown eyes, and he couldn't help smiling at her. She remained silent, but a wistful touch of humor deepened the single dimple in her cheek.

"Wiwilla," Conners said soberly. "I did a lot of thinking last night. I was so angry at losing you I was sick with it. But there's something else. Maybe Blackhorn's not so far wrong, maybe I don't have a right to drag you into my trouble. . . ."

She stopped him by bringing a soft pressure with her fingers on his lips. "Do you believe that when two people marry that all trouble in the world goes away? Do you think, if we didn't have this trouble, there wouldn't be other trouble? I've lived a long time with Blackhorn. I know what it's like to live in danger."

"It's not just that. I don't have a job. How will we live?"

"You don't have a house, and white men think houses are so important," she said, and suddenly she seemed far older and wiser than her years. "And you don't have any money, and white men think money is even more important than houses. But what kind of trouble is that? The only kind of house Blackhorn ever had is one like that shack where we wintered, and he's never had any money, except what he could steal, or get from trapping or hunting. If we let something little like that stop us, we'll never get married." She paused, moving back, away from him. "Or, maybe you've changed your mind, Conners. Maybe you want me to go back to Blackhorn."

"No. I can't do that, Wiwilla."

"Conners . . . then, do you love me?"

He did not speak, but took her in his arms again and kissed her. It was strange. He had always felt so awkward around other girls, like Opal, and now it was so natural.

Wiwilla responded to him and Conners was embarrassed by his involuntary physical reaction to her.

"Wiwilla," he said, pulling back slightly, "we have to catch up with the wagon train. The sutler's wife told me about a town a day's ride south, Lander. The wagon train is heading for there. It's a big town, Wiwilla. There's sure to be a parson there."

He knew in that moment, even as he spoke, that they could build a new life together. He did have a definite fondness for cattle. "Takin' after his uncle Mart," his father used to say to his mother when Conners would mention it. Uncle Mart was his mother's brother, who had gone to Arizona years back. There was a strain between the two families. Uncle Mart, when he would occasionally write, would write to Conners, never to his sister or her husband. He would tell his nephew about the cattle business and how the only way for a man to work was from a saddle. To Uncle Mart, the man who pushed a plow was as lowdown as a worm beneath a wet rock. A year ago his mother had told him that Uncle Mart had died from a broken neck when a horse threw him. But all the things Uncle Mart had written to him now teemed in Conners's mind. Somehow they would make their way to Arizona. He was sure that some friend of his uncle would help him get a riding job. He could ride well, that was for certain, and he was a middling roper.

They'd put this north country behind them. He could push from his mind all thought of vengeance, of being good with a gun, of going up against MacLane and his men. They could take a new name, he and Wiwilla, and with a new name and in a place far from this one, no one would ever find them. . . .

As it turned out, the wagon train hadn't gotten very far south of Fort Washakie. There were twenty big Murphy wagons in the train that had hauled freight on a government contract to the fort and were now returning empty to Fort Lincoln. Conners caught up with the wagon boss, who remembered that the sutler had spoken about him. He gave Conners the job of wrangling the stock and Wiwilla was able to hitch a ride on one of the wagons. She tied the mule behind the great Murphy.

It proved a long, monotonous drive, the mountains to their right flank always towering, the glaciers still glistening on their peaks. In the late afternoon, after crossing a river called the Popo Agie, its waters glutted by spring floods, but not so much as to be unnavigable, the train camped on the outskirts of Lander. Conners had to help unhitch and herd the mules. Once the stock was grazing, one of the teamsters took his place so Conners could go to the cook fire and get something to eat. Despite the exhaustion he felt, Conners had little appetite and he noticed that Wiwilla had not touched her food much, either. He went to the wagon boss and asked for a four-bit advance from him. When he learned what it was for, the wagon boss smiled and gave Conners the money.

Lander was a little, one-gallus town with dust caking the windows so thickly the setting sun didn't even glare off them. Dust lying in cornstarch drifts along the high, wooden curbs was stirred up by the slightest movement until it shrouded the street in a bank of yellow haze higher than a man's waist. Conners rode the Crazy Moon horse, Wiwilla the calico mule. After making an inquiry, Conners located a hardshell Baptist minister who lived in a shake house inappropriately next door to one of the larger saloons in town. The minister said his usual fee for weddings or funerals was a dollar, but when Conners rang the four-bit piece down onto the table, the man thought for a moment, then conceded that he might be able to do it at a lesser rate, seeing that the two of them were so young.

When they emerged from the brief ceremony, the sun had almost set and the shadows of the buildings lay like streaks of brown smoke across the streets. They did not ride; instead they led their mounts slowly down the street, heading in the direction of the camp. Conners stole a sidelong glance at Wiwilla. There was the faintest smile on her lips and her eyes were bright.

Conners cleared his throat. "Do you feel any different, Wiwilla?"

Her face turned away so that all he could see was the soft curve of her cheek. The dying sun lighted them in a hazy red glow.

"I don't feel too much different," she said, placing her fingers tightly on his arm.

"When I got the money, I told the wagon boss not to tell anyone. I figgered they'd want to throw a big doings and make an almighty whoop-te-doo. I told him we didn't want that. He said we could bed down in the number-two wagon."

They were at the edge of town now, and they left the road and crossed the fields, heading toward the wagon corral. The only noise behind them was the creak of a big hay wagon pulling into town; one of the mules snorted. The sound scarcely carried an echo.

"Conners," the girl said softly.

"Yes."

"I'd like to ask you something."

"Sure. What?"

"Is it true that among your people—"

"Don't say it that way, Wiwilla. Blackhorn drove it into you that you are a squaw, but you're as much white as you are Indian. You can be whatever you please."

Her eyes turned toward the ground. But her fingers tightened around his. "Well . . . ," she began again, softly, "among . . . I mean, when a white man gets married . . . does he carry his wife in the door of their house . . . that is, if they have one?"

"You mean, over the threshold," Conners said, laughing. "Ma told me Pa did it."

"Then I would like you to do that with me."

"But we ain't got no threshold, Wiwilla."

"A wagon tongue will do," she said. "I think being carried over a threshold in that kind of ceremony would make me feel married, really married, in a way that that parson didn't make me feel married."

Light was failing swiftly when they reached camp. Dusk was a sooty veil that made the wagons loom dimly. A few campfires were still going, but most of the teamsters were already rolled up in their blankets, sleeping beneath the wagons. The wagon boss had been true to his word; there would be no shindig. Conners paused with Wiwilla by the number-two wagon.

"I don't guess we had better sleep underneath," he said. His voice was muffled and he felt awkward. Wiwilla was silent but Conners knew she was looking at him, and while he couldn't see the expression on her face he knew she was gazing at him with the same solemn, quiet glance as she had so often before and which he found now so deeply stirring. "There's some wild hay inside," he said then. "The wagonmaster told me to gather it this afternoon before we went into town and he even lent me an old blanket. It'll make a good bed for us."

She did not speak, but her hand was very warm as he disengaged his hand from hers and took the reins of the calico mule from her other hand. He led the horse and mule to the front wheel on the left side of the wagon and hitched them there. He knew he should unsaddle them, but he couldn't, not now, his hands were trembling so. He cursed himself soundlessly.

"Wiwilla," he said, and his voice was so choked it barely came out.

"Yes," she answered.

She had been right behind him and he had not realized

how closely she was standing to him. Her voice sounded husky, not at all like a girl's voice now. The scent of her suddenly engulfed him, musky, wild, a little smoky, yet like sunlight and wind, as if such things could have a scent. He reached out toward her and she came heavily against him, holding his face between her long, slender fingers, pulling his lips down to hers. A pounding began inside him, a strangled feeling in his chest.

"Wiwilla," he said. "Wiwilla . . ."

He picked her up in his arms and carried her to the wagon tongue, where it rested against the earth, and stepped across it, careful in the darkness not to take a misstep. It had seemed like just a silly, girlish notion when she had asked it of him, but now he understood what it meant to her. It changed something inside her. He could feel it as he held her. It sealed something.

"I wish there was a door," he said, still carrying her, moving alongside the wagon until they reached the rear pucker and open back. He put her down inside and she held his hand, drawing him up and beside her, as they collapsed gently onto the wild hay with its blanket cover.

She had never called him anything else but Conners, until that night, when they were making love for the third time, she gasped his name, called him Gordon, and held him tightly to her. Then she lay softly curled next to him, sleeping, holding his right hand in both of hers. Conners felt an overwhelming sense of languor. He might have been asleep, too, but he couldn't be sure. His keen hearing had probably wakened him.

It had been a dull, clinking sound, like a bit chain, or the chain on a spur. It was repeated, nearer now. It made Conners pull himself away from Wiwilla and sit up, listening. Then Wiwilla was sitting up, too, just in front of him, looking, he thought, toward him, when the flash and roar came simultaneously. Not until he felt Wiwilla's body jerk, slamming into him, did he realize it was a shot. The impact knocked him backward, more deeply into the wild hay, and that was what saved his life. The gun exploded again. Conners felt the slug whip past him, hitting the panel of the wooden wagon bed in front.

He rolled over, covering Wiwilla's body with his own, when a third slug hit the floor of the wagon in front of his face, spewing tiny bits of straw into his open eyes, blinding him as much as the flash had. The camp was suddenly awake, men shouting, scrambling from under the wagons. One of the teamsters must have seen that last gun flash because he began firing in the direction of the rear of the wagon. Conners heard a figure dark in shadow near the tail-gate gasp, wheel, and fade quickly into the night. A moment later Conners could hear the sound of a horse running.

"Quit shooting!" Conners yelled frantically. "It's too late!"

The firing stopped. The greasy smell of spent gunpowder hung in the air, stifling Conners, as he reached outward for Wiwilla. If only she hadn't sat up, coming between him and the bullet that was meant for him.

The wagonmaster stood just outside the pucker in the rear now, holding a flaming torch. As the wavering circle of light flickered across Wiwilla's face, Conners could see that she wasn't looking up at him. The front of her dress was soaked with blood, crimson turning almost black, viscid, spreading. Then her eyes opened, looking up at him as he held her.

"In my heart . . . Gordon . . . in my heart . . . I am glad," she breathed, then her eyes closed again. Her body was damp with perspiration, and even as he held her, now so silent, she began to turn cold.

The wagonmaster had climbed onto the tailgate and now crept inside. He was still holding the flaming torch.

"I think it's over, son," he said.

★ ★ ★

At dawn, a mist rose off the river, fogging the bottomland timber and turning everything the color of old ashes. Conners had wept and held Wiwilla's body for a long time, his frame convulsed with sobs. The wagonmaster and the teamsters had left him alone in his grief, but they later offered to help when Conners had taken a shovel and gone to dig her grave. He had refused their offer.

Later, with the growing light, Conners was able to locate where, on the edge of the campground, a horse had been left with trailing reins while its master had crept quietly into camp in order to kill a girl. Conners noted the imprint of a star in the heel of the murderer's boots, and the difference in the two sets of tracks. The murderer had walked slowly into camp, stalking his enemy, while the tracks leading back to the horse were wider apart, made by a man obviously running.

Conners followed the tracks of the horse for a dozen yards, until the mount and rider had cut toward a bushy hill. He noted the direction the rider had taken, but it told him nothing. He must face this man. Even when the old sickness began to churn within him, he could feel it ebb when he thought of that confrontation. He would face him with a steady hand, and he would send a bullet into the man's stomach so that he would die slowly, so slowly that he would have time to tell him about Wiwilla, about the girl he had killed who had never done anything, who had been innocent and who deserved a good life, better even than what he could ever have given her, and who was now without any life at all.

The crowd of teamsters seemed to float in the gray vacuum of the mist. Some of them, including the wagonmaster, had paid their respects at Wiwilla's grave and the wagonmaster had said a few words over her which he read from a Bible. One of the teamsters had spat and called Conners a squawman. Conners had felt a sudden rage against the man, but, later, he wondered what his life with

Wiwilla really would have been like surrounded by men who felt that way.

Conners was back at the grave site, shivering in the cold mist, when the wagonmaster returned.

"You still coming with us, son?" he asked.

"No."

"Want I should send someone to town to fetch that parson and make all this more official?"

"I haven't any money."

Conners had not even looked at the wagonmaster. It was only when he heard his steps retreating that he looked up and saw that he had left a wooden headboard behind and, on top of it, a double eagle. Conners was on his feet then, ready to run after the man, not to thank him, but to give it all back to him. Something held him fast. He could hear the horse he had ridden and the calico mule nearby, cropping at the buffalo grass, loosely tethered by one of the teamsters. It was matted turf, going to seed now, straw-colored from curing all summer long in the hot sun. He was standing there, still undecided about what to do, when he heard the creak of a saddle. He turned to see a rider at the edge of the clearing. When he had first heard the sound, he had thought it was probably a teamster, but now he knew it wasn't. It was Blackhorn. He had one of his Navy Colts drawn, pointed at Conners.

He felt neither surprise nor fear. He felt nothing.

"If you think I deserve killing," Conners said, "go ahead and drop the hammer."

Blackhorn did not reply. He continued to hold the gun on Conners, one twisted, rheumatic thumb hooked over the big, single-action hammer. His face was half-buried in the curly mat of his hair and beard, appearing like the mane of an old, mangy lion, frosted gray, filthy with bear grease, buffalo fur, wild hay, and whatever else blew on the wind snarled in the ghastly strands. The seams in his cheeks were deep with grime, beneath ice-colored eyes, blank and glittering, more than a little savage. He remained seated on one of the Crazy Moon horses and his hand began to tremble in an involuntary palsy. Conners was certain he was going to fire. Then a broken sound came from him. The gun sank against his saddle and he bowed his head.

"I wish I could kill you, son," he said. "I wish to God I could."

Something cracked open inside Conners, like a wound opening up, and all his pent-up grief and guilt began to hemorrhage, tears streaming down his shattered face. "I didn't have no right to take her, Blackhorn. I just as well killed her myself. She was the best thing we ever had, either of us. Maybe you treated her like dirt sometimes, but I killed her. I—" His voice broke. "I am a Jonah, just like you said I was."

"Booger! You was born under a dark cloud. Yeah, you're a Jonah all right, to man or woman."

Blackhorn's head began shaking back and forth. It was a slow, strange movement, as though he no longer had control over it, shaking back and forth, on and on. He climbed off the horse, his head still shaking, then leaned against the animal, his face touching the worn saddle. He stood there like that, for a long time, a man exhausted to the point of collapse. Finally he pulled himself away from the horse and shuffled to the other end of a deadfall, sitting down on the rotted trunk. His elbows were now on his knees, the gun dangling from one hand. Conners had never seen him look so old. When Blackhorn did speak, it was little more than a feeble croaking.

"It wouldn't do no good to kill you," he said. "God damn you, it wouldn't do no good."

"But you think it's what I got coming." The way he said it, it was a statement.

"She made the choice, Conners. She come back to you. The man that needs killing is the one that's been following me all these years and now is following you, the man with the star in his boot heel."

"It was dark. All I saw was a shadow. A big shadow."

"Some Indians camped yonder said they saw a white man come riding from this direction last night."

Conners's mouth hardened. The tears had stopped. "Blackhorn, I want to do it. I want to kill him."

"What?"

"The man who killed Wiwilla. I want to kill him. And the man who hired him."

"You wouldn't stand a chance."

"Maybe." He gave a short laugh. Conners's face looked older. "I figgered me and Wiwilla would go to Arizona. I used to have an uncle there in the cattle business. I had our life all figgered out. I was going to forget MacLane and everything that had happened to my folks. I figgered to turn my back on all of it and make me and Wiwilla a new life."

"Plans ain't no good, son. A man lives from one sunup to the next." His head was no longer shaking. He glared sharply at Conners. "She was only fourteen years old. That's all. Just fourteen."

"I'm going back to Table Rock, and when I do, I'll have a gun in my hand."

"One gunshot and you'll head for the brush."

"You can help me get past that." Conners looked imploringly at the seamed old face.

"I might at that," he said, holding Conners's gaze. "It'll take time. I'll do it. But we got to agree on one thing. I'm not doing it for you. I'm doing it for Willa. And I don't never want you to mention her name to me, not never. If you do, I'll get to thinking about her, lying cold in the ground, and there's no telling what I'd likely do."

Conners turned to the headpost on the ground behind him. He removed the double eagle and put it in his pocket.

"Use my skinning knife and cut her name deep," Blackhorn said, still seated on the rotted trunk. It was the last thing he said to Conners that day.

CHAPTER 8

UNDER THE IMPETUS of cattle and the railroad, coal and gold, Table Rock had blossomed into a boomtown of major proportions in the five years since Bob Conners was hanged. The original town, lying in the hollow beneath the great hanging rock, was now the main business district with the biggest, most expensive saloons and hotels, the banks, the railroad yards, all crowded into a little area only four blocks long and three wide. From this, the streets spread over a dozen hills, haphazard, winding lanes lined for the most part with squalid little miners' shacks. A dozen coal mines operated right in among them, and the dank, empty adits of old, worked-out lodes scarred the hills and gaped in many of the backyards.

Coming in from the south, a man had to follow the trail through Chinatown before reaching the main part of town. This had grown, too, with the Chinese labor brought in to work for the railroad and in the mines, until there was close to a thousand people in Chinatown.

The two men riding in that day did not cause any special notice. One was very old and seamed, in rawhide clothes of incredible filth, sitting his horse in a humped, delicate way, as if each movement of the ancient, crow-bait horse caused him pain. The other was young and tall, with a long, finely chiseled face thrown into shadow by his hat-brim. The only broad part about him was his shoulders, and their breadth was given even more accent by the contrast of his narrow hips and waist. He wore a black frock coat that fell in folds over the handle of a gun at his right side. Gordon Conners was five years removed from the boy who had left town after his father had been hanged.

The changes that had come with manhood had not robbed him of his strange, acutely perceptive senses. The babble, the smells, the color, the constant movement of Chinatown beat against him in a sharply defined series of pictures that never ceased to engage his attention. His eyes moved quickly, incessantly, taking in one sight after another. He did not miss a movement, a glance, a facial expression, and they all had their meaning for him. His ears seemed to catch every word, English or Chinese, that was spoken on the flimsy, wooden sidewalks flanking the street. He caught the scent of roast pig and almond duck and chop suey on the same breath, then the reek of garbage and rotting clothes and burned firecrackers that littered the gutters.

"Thanks for sticking with me, Blackhorn," Conners said.

"We got Willa right here beside us, son."

"We're through running. If it's true Roland Bayard has coal on that land he and dad were working, I'm entitled to half of it by inheritance. We've tried every other way to cure your rheumatism there is. Money's the only thing that'll get us a doctor who can cure you now."

Blackhorn nodded, but they both knew that his rheumatism wasn't the only reason they were doing this. A lot of traveling lay behind them. Arizona. New Mexico. California. Mexico. They had not come across the man with the star in his boot heels again during those years, but there had been others, all dead now, so Connors and Blackhorn knew they were still in his tally book. And always, along that trail, the wish to return had been in Conners, an insistent, abiding wish, sometimes dim, sometimes strong, compounded of many other wishes—the wish to end their furtive running, to find who had murdered his father and mother and why, to claim whatever inheritance he had from the estate his father had left.

And besides that was something even more defined, a fugitive memory, coming back smokily. None of the women along the way could obliterate her memory. It was as if, as Blackhorn had said, she was right there alongside them. At Lander, they had stopped at Wiwilla's grave. Wild flax was blooming on it like chips of fallen sky. Conners had closed his eyes and her face had appeared before him and he could feel her trembling in his arms. Wiwilla. Spirit of the Spring . . .

A series of crackling explosions snapped Conners out of his reverie, and he pulled his horse up sharply. Then he saw that it was only firecrackers thrown by the Chinese. An immense dragon was winding itself down the street, bending back and forth. It must have been a hundred feet long, with men inside at intervals of every few feet, their legs moving grotesquely beneath the rippling green silk of the sides. The head was set with long, curving horns, and a pronged tongue was thrust from its red, gaping mouth. Its bulging eyes were red and green, rolling lecherously at the crowd. At every house of business, the dragon stopped, its head turned toward the sidewalk, to bow in sinuous obeisance to the vivid ideograph papers pasted on the flimsy walls.

The shouting, hooting crowd pressed against Conners's horse, forcing it over to the sidewalk, almost onto a man who stood among the onlookers. Fighting the excited horse, Conners only half-saw the man, realizing that he was a white.

"What's going on," he asked, when the animal was in hand.

"Oh, one of their damn celebrations. They seem to have one every few days—"

The abrupt way the man stopped brought Conners's attention back to him. It was the first time Conners had looked directly at his face. It was Rodger MacLane.

Both men stared for a long, speechless moment at each

other, neither trying to hide his surprise. MacLane had changed a little. His head was a little whiter, a leonine mane of prematurely turned hair, accentuating the ruddy flush of good living in his heavy-fleshed face. Conners had wondered many times what he would feel if he ever met any of these men again. He had expected hate, with MacLane, or rage, instant and blinding, bringing a violent need to get his hands on the man.

But it was not coming that way. There was a sense of antagonism, deep and intense. No denying that. But the rest of his feeling remained within him, turgid and obscure, stirring like something long asleep down in his depths.

"I guess I'd better look at who I speak to in Table Rock, after this," Conners said at last.

"You've changed," MacLane said. "I'd hardly recognize you."

The voice did it. The deep, husky voice Conners had heard outside the sod house that day took him back on a sweeping, giddy tide, with the memory of his father swinging from the poplar, and his mother's feeble, dying body stirring restlessly beneath the covers. He found the feeling more definable within him now.

"I would recognize you, MacLane. I'd never forget you."

The ruddy flush paled from the leathery, weathered flesh of MacLane's face, leaving it a strange, putty color. He had been standing with his hands in his pockets, the tails of his steel-pen coat pushed back. He took his hands out now, carefully, so that the coattail still hung free of his gun butt.

"Is that what you came back for?" he asked.

Conners reined in his fiddling horse, aware that Blackhorn was in front of him, against the curb, watching all this closely from the back of his own nag.

"I came back for a lot of things, MacLane," Conners said.

Beside MacLane stood a wizened, subservient man with a slack-lipped, undershot jaw and eyes that kept moving incessantly. He had been tugging at MacLane's sleeve like a peevish child.

"Who is it, Rodger?" he kept asking. "Who is it?"

"Shut up, Faro," said MacLane, trying to shrug him loose.

"Who is it?"

"It's Gordon Conners," MacLane said in a loud voice.

"Gordon Conners." There was a strange, whispered awe in the man's pasty face as he stared up at Conners.

"You're a damn fool to come back at all," MacLane said to Conners in a loud, pompous way. "Nobody's forgotten, Conners. A rustler's still a rustler."

This brought the anger Conners had waited for. He felt his hands close viciously on the saddle horn, with a small, muted popping of bones and tendons. He knew now that if MacLane made one move, those hands would be on the man. He welcomed it, in a strange, savage way. He bent toward MacLane, and his voice held a faint tremor as he spoke.

"That's right, MacLane. Nobody's forgotten. In fact, you remember Tom Union?"

"What about him? He disappeared a few years back."

"He used to work for you, didn't he?"

"No. He never worked for me. What does it matter?"

"The past matters a lot, MacLane," said Conners. He stared at the man till MacLane's gaze broke, darting in a fluttering, guilty way to Blackhorn.

"Damn you," he blustered. "You'd better not stay here, Conners. That's all. You'd better not stay here."

He whirled and pushed his way through the thinning crowd. Faro continued to stare up at Conners. His mouth began to twitch. Then it formed a slack, foolish grin, and he turned to walk idly down Teton Avenue, pushed this way and that by the celebrating Orientals. Conners, however, was still looking after MacLane.

"So that's the man who hung your father," muttered Blackhorn.

"You know him?" said Conners.

"Not aside from what I've heard about him," said Blackhorn. "I wouldn't have needed that, to know who he was. You looked ready to jump down his throat."

Conners stared at his hands on the saddle horn. They hurt when he released his grip. "Did it show that much?"

"It scared me," said Blackhorn. "I never saw you look so mean before."

Conners shrugged, turning up on Teton. Here, on the border of Chinatown, was a rooming house for white miners that Conners remembered as being cheap and fairly reputable. They took a double, bathed, and ate. After the meal, Blackhorn's rheumatism bothered him so much he went to bed. Conners wanted to see Bayard, and Blackhorn told him to go ahead.

His black horse, Spades, was still jaded from the long ride behind them, but it was too far to walk. Conners had found out that Bayard kept offices in the Union Pacific building at Fourth and Teton, a three-story brick structure with the Table Rock Bank in the first story. Conners hitched Spades to a hitch rail, seeing more than one Crazy Moon on the rumps of the other horses there. Bayard's suite was on the second floor, boasting a sumptuous waiting room that buzzed with a sense of subdued activity. There was a desk to one side of a door marked "Roland Bayard, Private." Secretaries emerged frequently from this door with their hands full of papers, disappearing through another door. At the desk was a small, mousy, bald man, checking some kind of list.

"I'd like to see Roland Bayard," Conners told him.

"Mr. Bayard is not in right now," said the man without looking up.

"I saw him through that door," Conners said.

The man raised condescending eyes to him. "I said Mr. Bayard is not in right now."

"Tell him Gordon Conners would like to see him."

"You can leave your name."

"You can take it in to him right now."

The man smiled and shifted his leg a little beneath the desk. Then he lowered his head and started writing again. Face tightening angrily, Conners started to speak again, when the door opened behind him.

"This is Mr. Conners," said the clerk without raising his head from the list. "He won't believe Mr. Bayard is not in."

Conners turned to see that a big redheaded man had stepped through the door, closing it behind him. He had a freckled, heavy-framed face, the prominence of his cheekbones darkened and accentuated by old bruises. His stiff white collar cut into the flesh of an immensely muscled neck, and his single-breasted coat was drawn out of fit by the bulge of his beefy shoulders and the harnessed gun under one arm. His bland smile flashed square, chalky teeth, broken and chipped across the front.

"You'd better take Harry's word for it, friend," he said. "When Mr. Bayard ain't in, he ain't in."

It had taken Conners this long to recognize the man. "Perhaps you didn't catch the name, Halleck. Gordon Conners."

Jack Halleck's smile disappeared. His head thrust itself forward on that thick, swollen neck. "Gordon Conners!" he said. Then he began to chuckle. It held a sarcastic tone. "I guess I didn't catch the name at that, did I? It was so completely beyond anything I'd expected. A bolt out of the blue you might say. Little Gordon Conners come back to his hometown at last. That's too bad, Gordon. I'll tell

Roland you were here when he comes back. He'll be sorry he missed you."

Conners had been containing himself with some effort. His voice had a thin, strained sound. "Look, Halleck, I'm tired of this runaround. I know Roland's in there and I know he'd see me if he knew I was here. Now have the decency to go in and tell him."

"Sure I'll tell him, Gordon," grinned Halleck. "When he gets back."

Conners felt his hands drawing into fists and straightened them out with effort. "Then I'm going in myself, Halleck. Will you step aside."

"I'll escort you out, Gordon."

"In," said Conners.

"Out," said Halleck, taking a step forward and reaching for Conners's arm to spin him around.

Conners wasn't there.

Surprise turned Halleck's face blank as his arm was caught from the side, where Conners had stepped. He was spun, instead of Conners, around against the desk, so hard it skidded back into the clerk, knocking him over backward in his chair. Conners's face was a mask of deliberate, controlled anger as he stepped into Halleck without giving him a chance to recover. Off-balance against the sliding desk, Halleck tried to regain his footing, throwing up one thick, hairy arm.

Conners caught it with his left hand, tearing it aside, and sunk his right deep into that beefy belly. Halleck doubled over and spun away sideways from the desk, still trying to fend Conners off with his feebly swinging arm. Conners caught it once more, pulling the man around so he could hit him in the face.

Halleck was square, with his back toward the outer door, and he staggered backward, his head jerked upward by the blow, finally to lose footing in the hallway. He fell heavily, sliding against the opposite wall. Conners had followed as far as the door, to see if that was the end of it. Halleck made an effort to rise, then slumped back against the wall, groaning.

Some faint, hissing movement of cloth down the hall brought Conners's attention that way. It seemed as if nothing had changed. For a moment, he wasn't in this building, a man, with all that behind him. He was in the glade, by the pool, with only Opal Hamilton there. Her hair yellow as ripe corn. The grave wide-set eyes, deep as the pool. The body, in cashmere now, instead of crinoline, shimmering on the deep outward curve of breast, forming a sharp highlight across the swell of hip.

"Gordon!" she said, in a throaty, shocked tone.

He removed his hat and bowed, without smiling. "Miss Hamilton."

As she came toward him the whisper of cloth against her moving body stirred something in him, the way it had so long ago. But it was no longer indefinable, as it had been then. She looked at Halleck, still on the floor, a puzzled frown marring her brow. Then she turned back to Conners, catching at his wrist in that characteristic gesture.

"Gordon!" she said again, in that blank, unbelieving way, with something else mixed in, a question, a dark wonder. "You've come back for revenge."

"Maybe."

"I have a feeling you would have killed Jack Halleck if he said he was a party to that shooting at the dugout—"

"Opal, you don't understand. My ma and pa . . . I have their blood on my hands."

"You've changed, Gordon." She touched his holstered gun with the tip of a forefinger. "You've conquered your fear of guns, haven't you?"

He nodded. "I can stand up to the sound of a gun without going to pieces."

"Don't change, Gordon. Don't change too much." She

touched his arm with her gloved hand. "If MacLane is guilty, he should pay for it. But not by destroying you."

"You might as well know something, Opal. I . . . I was married."

Her mouth opened slowly and she took her hand from his arm.

"An Indian girl up at Lander." It still hurt him to talk about it. "On our wedding night, she was shot. I was holding her in my arms, and MacLane's man killed her."

She made a soft, little sound in the shadows. "Gordon, I didn't realize. I'm . . . I'm so sorry."

"Gordon Conners!" echoed someone from behind, and he half-turned to see Roland Bayard filling the doorway to the office. Conners turned back to Opal.

"I have business now, Opal, if you'll excuse me. I'd like to see you afterward."

"My home. This evening. Dinner?"

"I have a friend."

"Bring him."

"Thank you."

As she turned to go, she cast another look at Halleck, and that same dark, wondering frown touched her brow once more. It disturbed Conners. Then he was turning around to receive Bayard's greeting, vivid and warm as the man himself.

"I won't apologize about your muscleman," Conners told him, as Bayard ushered him into the inner sanctum. "Halleck . . ."

"Halleck?" Bayard grinned. "Forget it. I have to keep a couple of them around to shoo away the flies. You know how it is in this business."

"No," said Conners. "How is it?"

Baynard's smile faded a little, as he closed the door behind him with a muted click. "What do you mean, Gordon?"

"Just that." Conners shrugged. "My rights of inheritance

entitle me to half of whatever you get off the Harrison Basin properties, don't they?"

"Of course, Gordon, of course. I didn't know where to get in touch with you—" Bayard broke off, turning to the other men in the room. There were four of them standing, a trio of Chinese, in the traditional silk jackets and conical hats, their almond eyes regarding Conners with bland curiosity. The fourth was big for an Oriental, nearly six feet tall, dressed in a well-tailored sack coat, the impeccable cut failing to hide shoulders of remarkable size. His eyes lacked the slant of the Chinese, and even had a pronounced Caucasian lid. But there was something disturbingly Oriental about his eyes; they seemed to stare beyond the confines of this room, in dreamy thought, holding unreadable, unplumbed depths.

"This is the son of my dead partner, Gordon Conners," Bayard said, introducing them. "Gordon, this is Cheney Lee."

The light shifted across the raw, Mongoloid surfaces of Cheney Lee's face in a flutter of changing planes as he inclined his head. "I have heard of you, Mr. Conners," he said, in excellent English.

"Can we put this off till tomorrow, now, Lee?" asked Bayard. "I haven't seen Gordon in years, and I'd like to talk with him."

Lee's voice lowered to hissing, sibilant tones. "My people have been put off too long already, Mr. Bayard. Tomorrow may be too late. Rumblings were heard in many of the houses along Peking Alley yesterday. You know that more than one mine tunnel is dug beneath those streets. If something is not done at once about filling them up, the whole of Peking Alley may cave in, and cause many deaths."

"But the railroad doesn't have control—"

"The railroad knew those houses were condemned when they bought them for their Chinese labor," said Cheney

Lee. "Ever since that joss house on Lotus Flower Lane caved in and the baby was killed, there has been much ill feeling in Chinatown. The treatment your people have given mine through the years has not helped. If another of those cave-ins occurs, you're liable to have a riot on your hands. We want your word that you will do something about it."

"All right," said Bayard, moving his hand in an impatient gesture. "I'll see what I can do. But I want you to understand it's not my true res—"

"Not just like that," said Cheney Lee. "Not waving it away with your hand. I've seen you dispose of the problem that way too many times before."

The man in the leather armchair rose. He had been sitting there from the beginning, and Conners had noticed him when he first came in. But his silence, his lack of movement had been so complete that Conners had forgotten about him. He was tall, without breadth. His shoulders were hardly broader than his waist. Yet, the very singular narrowness of his whole frame lent it a strong force somehow—the sliding force of a serpent. His voice came from thin lips that hardly moved, in a sallow, ageless face.

"Mr. Bayard gave you his word," he said, softly. "He'd like you to leave, now."

Cheney Lee turned unhurriedly toward the man. "I will only dignify this once by speaking, Fontenelle. I told you before there was no point in my talking to Mr. Bayard's underlings. There is nothing you or I can say to each other."

Fontenelle's face remained expressionless before the almost palpable impact of those strange, ancient eyes. His own eyes caught the light in some small shift, glittering with the bright, blank opacity of chipped glass.

"There is something I can say to you," he murmured. "Get out."

Cheney Lee smiled. At least his lips pulled back until

they lay flat and tilted against his teeth. There was no humor in the rest of his face.

"Have you ever made issue with an Oriental before, Fontenelle?"

"There's always a first time."

"I am not really Oriental, you know." Cheney Lee smiled. "My father was an Irishman."

"You're still a Chink to me," said Fontenelle.

"Perhaps it is as well that you think of me that way," said Cheney Lee. "Then you will know the mistake it would be to cause me trouble. My ancestors were feeding bamboo shoots to their enemies before your ancestors were born. Do you know what that means, Fontenelle?"

"I don't even care."

"A small shoot of bamboo is rolled into a meatball, or baked into a meatball, or baked in a biscuit. It unrolls in the stomach. The intestine is cut to bits. It is a very agonizing death, Fontenelle. Think about it the next time you eat. I know many cooks in your part of town . . ."

Still smiling, Cheney Lee bowed. When he lifted his head, he was turned toward Conners. Some small alteration of expression passed through his eyes. Then he had turned to lead the other bowing Chinese out of the room.

Bayard stared after the receding sound of their feet, until it had died outside. There was a tight, studying expression on his face. His head twitched a little, as if it were surprised to remember Conners was still in the room. He turned with an apologetic shrug.

"Thank you, Fontenelle," he said. "Will you wait outside now?"

The narrow man looked at him. "You sure?"

"Yes, yes," Bayard said in a harried way. Fontenelle turned and moved with that utterly silent, sinuous lack of effort toward the door. The motion caused his eyes to pass across Conners's, before their focus was carried to the door. For just that moment, with their two gazes meeting,

Conners thought he caught some fugitive expression behind the chipped-glass blankness in Fontenelle's eyes.
Then it was gone, and the door was closing after the man.

"Another fly swatter?" asked Conners.

"Charlie Fontenelle," said Bayard. "You'll come to ap-
preciate him if you're around long."

"I plan to be around," said Gordon. "I don't mean to
just step in and claim my half without putting anything in,
Roland. I realize you've worked hard to develop what
you've got here."

Bayard nodded, running a hand through his hair. It
had been so vivid and black once; it was shot with gray
now, thinning at the back of the skull. He paced to the
window, stared out.

"We found the coal about a year ago, Gordon. After that
rustling trouble, your father's death, the feeling around
here, I couldn't come back. I waited a long time at Bannerman's line cabin for you. Finally I trailed for Cheyenne. I hired a man there to work the Harrison Basin
place for me. He came across the coal. It made me big
enough to buck what I would meet, coming back here. My
connection with the railroad helped, too. They leased the
land, put me in charge of all their coal mines around
here."

"Anything I can do to make me worthwhile?"

Bayard nodded. "Matter of fact, there is. I've got a lot
of other interests around Table Rock besides mining, Gordon. I'm still a cattleman, essentially, and there's still a lot
of the Harrison Basin Ranch that isn't being worked for
coal. Remember that idea your father and I had about
breeding up the stock with English imports? I've been
trying to build a herd that way, but MacLane and the cattle
crowd still have it in for me. They're doing everything they
can to hamstring the job. I need a man out there I can
trust."

He turned almost sheepishly to Conners. "Matter of

fact, Gordon, word has sort of leaked back about you. That affair in Arizona. The business in California. If I hadn't heard things like that, I wouldn't suggest the job to you. You are still awfully young, and it would be a big bite for the best. But what I heard convinces me you've learned to handle yourself in almost any situation. And you have been working cattle a lot along the trail, haven't you?"

"Enough," said Conners. "I'll take a whack at it if you want me to, Roland. Why don't we get started right now at this thing. I'd like to see your books and find out just where we stand. I realize my share won't all be in cash, but there must be some liquid assets, and I have a friend who needs some medical attention pretty bad."

Though Bayard was looking directly at Conners, his vivid, black eyes seemed to lose focus for an instant. "Sure, sure, Gordon," he said abruptly, and turned away in a nervous movement, running a hand through his rumpled hair again. "You'll have to wait a couple of days, though. The U. P. examines the books every year, and they've got them down at Laramie."

"Why should they take them way down there?"

"Just their way, just their way," said Bayard. He turned back swiftly, holding his hand out to Conners. "If you want any cash, though, I'll be glad to advance you some against your share."

Conner's eyes narrowed in vague speculation, attempting to define what was really going on. "Actually, Roland, what am I worth?"

Roland shrugged, seated himself at the desk, and opened a cigar box. "It would be hard to tell, Gordon."

Conners declined the cigar. "Surely, you've kept better records than that."

The man fumbled his own cigar, getting it from the box. It slipped from his fingers and rolled onto the floor. He bent to retrieve it with a sharp, guilty motion.

"It's mushroomed so fast, Gordon," he said, raising up

with a grunt. "You can understand that. You're big. I'll tell you that. You're big."

Conners came over to the desk, bending toward Bayard. "Roland, what's the matter?"

Bayard looked up at him, a lighted match held to his cigar. "Nothing, Gordon. We'll straighten it out, as soon as the books are back. I've been awfully busy. You understand that. We'll straighten it out."

"Will we, Roland?" asked Conners softly.

CHAPTER 9

OPAL HAMILTON'S PLACE was a neat white cottage out on Harrison Basin Road, set back in a grove of poplars, filling the night with their spring tang. When Conners had left, five years ago, she had shared the home with her mother; but her mother had since died, and Opal was alone now. They had a supper of chicken and mashed potatoes and apple pie; Blackhorn left soon after, saying he had eaten too much. Conners felt obligated to go with him, but the old man would not hear of it. Conners, a worried frown on his face, watched him ride off down the road.

"You're as bad as a hen with her chicks," smiled Opal. "Is it only his rheumatism?"

He turned to her. "What do you mean?"

She shrugged, turning to pile up the dirty plates. "He mentioned that he knew your father before you settled here in Table Rock. It's tied up with your father's death, somehow, isn't it? There are a lot of folks in town still wonder about that, Gordon. Your dad wasn't the kind to rustle stock. Why should someone want to get rid of him?"

He was impelled to move to the table, staring across it at her. "Seems to me you know a lot."

"I know you didn't come back just because Blackhorn needed medical attention," she said.

"There were a lot of things pulling me . . . Opal," he said, looking into her eyes.

"Like wanting to find out who had your dad killed . . . and why?"

"Isn't that a natural desire?"

"I don't know," she said. "It might be. I can't see you

feeling too deeply about it. You and your dad were never close."

"Mother and I were," he said. "Whoever framed Dad killed her just as sure as if they'd pulled the trigger."

"You sound vindictive."

"Wouldn't you be?"

"It's so different from what you used to be," she said. "I remember when you cried because Jack Halleck killed a pigeon in the schoolyard, and then you flew into a rage."

"And got the stuffing beat out of me," he said.

"Were you remembering that today when you whipped Halleck?"

He studied her face trying to find what was in her mind. "I was remembering a lot of things."

"Would you cry now if he killed a pigeon?"

Conners dropped his eyes to the table, smiled ruefully. "I don't think so."

"It's hard to believe you've changed so, in such a short time," she said. "You were an incredibly sensitive boy, so acutely attuned to the beauties of life, feeling actual physical pain at the sight of anything else suffering."

"A boy so sensitive you weren't sure whether or not he was actually a coward," he said. "Are you asking me to go back to that?"

"I don't think you could," she said. "You've lost so much of it. You've gone so far the other way. I think you actually enjoyed beating Halleck today."

"I was here in Table Rock almost five years as a kid, with Halleck around practically every day, baiting me, taunting me, goading me." He had wheeled from the table and was pacing nervously to the window. "That stays in a man's mind a long time."

"Did you feel the same way when you killed Tom Union?"

This caused him to wheel sharply toward her. "You know?"

"Word drifted back very soon after it happened," she said. "It gave you quite a reputation. Tom was known for how he could use a gun."

"And word came right back here . . . real quick, I bet," he said, thinking of the man with the star on his boot.

"Yes," she said. "How you'd killed a man."

He saw that she was not thinking of it in the same light as he was, and turned to walk toward her. "Quit trying to reconcile it, Opal. Can't you just accept it? The places I've been. The things I've had to do. The people I've been thrown in with—I couldn't have stayed alive five minutes as the boy you knew. It taught me in a few minutes what Dad had been trying to show me all my life without knowing how. Blackhorn was caught by a bear up in the Wind Rivers and would have been killed if I hadn't shot the bear. I did it without thinking. It was the only thing to do. Would you have me stand by and watch the bear tear him to shreds?"

"It isn't what you did, it's how you felt inside."

"I felt sick at first. Then I didn't feel anything. It's like cutting your finger. When you're a baby and do it, you get scared and bawl. When you get a little older you just go and bandage it up."

"A man's fingers can get so calloused by work that he no longer feels what he used to do with them."

"Does that make work bad?" he questioned. "If the fingers didn't get calloused, they'd be constantly hurt. It's the same way with the man, Opal. It was a hurt I felt over the pigeon, wasn't it? And I'd go on being hurt by things like that until I learned that they just had to be. Isn't that just growing up? I must have had it in me to change or I wouldn't have done it. What you saw was only a part of me."

"And now I can't see it at all," she said.

"Would you respect a coward, Opal?"

"I couldn't respect a killer, either. I saw it in you today, with Halleck. You whipped him vengefully, Gordon. And if you ever find the man who framed your father and caused your mother's death, whatever you did to him would be in vindication, calling up the same savage, bestial satisfaction that I saw in you today with Halleck."

He tried to recall his emotions with Halleck. Had they actually been that? Then he remembered MacLane, and how he had felt then. He shook his head.

"You're dramatizing it," he said. "I can do that, too. It isn't only my father whose life was threatened by this. Whoever was after him is after me, Opal. It's been hanging over my head ever since I left Table Rock."

In terse sentences, he told her of the holdup at Arapahoe Wells, and the rest of the story. She watched in an amazed, unbelieving way.

"I took it for granted the things that changed you weren't ordinary circumstances," she said. "I can see that you're fighting for your life."

"You might put it that way," he said. "Does that change the picture at all for you?"

"It might." She was studying him carefully. "And yet, Gordon, when it comes right down to it, could I be sure that a little of your motive, a lot of it, wasn't still revenge? Can you be sure yourself?"

He looked at her, but he was really looking at something within himself. "Would that be so wrong?" he said.

"Vengeance twists a man, Gordon. It does something inside. It grows into something small and mean and vicious that allows him to do just what you did today with Halleck."

"You're taking an awfully dim view."

"I have to," she said. "What I saw in you today frightened me, Gordon. If you can kill as easily and viciously as you whipped Halleck, it makes you something terrible—it makes you something even worse than most people, because your capacities extend so far beyond an ordinary man's."

"I see you've got it set in your mind that way, and all the talking we'd do in the world wouldn't change it," he said. "Maybe we've talked too much, Opal. What a woman feels for a man shouldn't come from the mind anyway."

He moved toward her as he said it. Her breasts lifted sharply with her inhalation, and she seemed about to step back.

He caught her in his arms before that impulse. The first contact inundated his senses with her. They seemed intensified even beyond their usual perception, drinking in the richness of her till it was as palpable as the taste of a heavy, sweet wine on his tongue. The hot, curved feel of her body against his. The silken warmth of her back beneath his hand. The throaty passion in the husky sound she made, as he put his lips to hers.

She seemed about to recoil, with one hand against his chest. Then her body relaxed against him. He had no measure of time.

When he finally released her, he was trembling all over. He had never thought it possible to desire something so much. They were both breathing in a heavy, shaken way.

"Gordon," she said, through faintly parted lips, staring up at him. "Gordon." In a soft, wondering way, and then her shining eyes darkened, and she took a step backward. She lowered her eyes to the table. "You *have* learned a lot while you were away."

"Maybe you won't feel such a great need to reconcile things now," he said, and brought himself in toward her again.

She stepped back. "No, Gordon," she said, sharply.

He halted, staring at her, a dozen things passing through his face, and his mind.

"There's something else besides just what's happened to me?" he asked.

"What do you mean?"

"You're a beautiful woman, Opal. There must have been other men during this time."

"There were," she said.

"There are?" he said.

She shrugged, turning away, in some withdrawal. "All right. There are."

"Are you in love?"

Her head snapped around, chin lifting. "Do you think I'd let you kiss me like that if I were?"

"I apologize," he said, inclining his head. "Maybe there's a special one, then. One you like more than the others."

"Isn't that my business?"

"Not unless you're putting me off completely," he said. "If you aren't, you know how I feel about you, and I think that entitles me to know where I stand. If vengeance is a small thing, Opal, so is coyness."

"All right," she said, with an angry toss of her head. "There are several I've been seeing. I like them all. Rodger MacLane's son, Todd. A man on the school board I'm thrown together with quite often. Another, named Cheney Lee—"

"Not that Chinaman!"

The shock in his voice brought her head around again. "He's not a Chinaman. He's a Eurasian. His father was an Irishman, his mother a Mongol slave brought over to California in the 1850s."

"And you see him?"

"You make it sound so awful. What's the matter with that? He's more of a gentleman than any other man in this town will ever be. He's educated, cultivated, kind."

"Are you in love with him?"

"You asked me that before."

"If you were in love with him, would you marry him?"

"What's wrong with that?"

"Yes," asked Cheney Lee from the doorway. "What's wrong with that?"

They both turned and saw him standing there. Opal had left the door ajar in the warmth of the night, and light from within made a shadowed, enigmatic mask of his face.

"Would you rather have me hypocritical or impolite, Opal?" he asked.

"Impolite, by all means, Cheney," she said.

"Then I will not pretend I did not overhear your conversation. I did not know you had company. I wouldn't have come to the door."

"Please come in," she said.

He moved into the living room with a sinuous lack of effort, smiling blandly at Conners. "There are many people in Table Rock prejudiced against the Chinese, Mr. Conners. From what I had heard of you, I hoped I would not number you among them."

"Perhaps the prejudice is more personal than racial," Conners told him.

"You object to my seeing Opal?"

"I guess I'd resent any man seeing Opal, white or red or black or yellow."

"This is nonsense," said Opal. "Won't you sit down, Cheney?"

"I won't intrude."

"You're a little late with that sentiment," said Conners.

Lee's smile made that bland enigma of his face again, lifting the oblique planes of his cheekbones till they almost hid his eyes. "You seem bent on making an issue of it, Mr. Conners. Have you ever made issue with an Oriental before?"

"I heard the speech you gave to Fontenelle."

"If the words are wise, they will bear repetition. I would advise you not to make an issue, Mr. Conners. There are so many things you don't know about us, and so many we do know about you."

Conners felt his head incline sharply toward the man. "Just how do you mean that?"

"If you are in town long enough, I am sure you will find out." Cheney Lee smiled softly.

Night turned the Harrison Basin road to a shadowy velvet tapestry. The brush and deeper timber were a depthless black, with the nearer trees forming a vague pattern of lighter hue. The road unfolded dimly beneath a cloud-obscured moon, winding away from Opal Hamilton's house toward town. Conners rode in bleak anger, unable to think of anything save what had happened back there. He had left Cheney Lee with Opal, seeing no point in continuing the still reserve that had stifled even the most meager conversation as Opal served coffee. He found himself seething with the desire to strike out at the man somehow, just to get his hands on him. He realized how childish that was. Then the deeper implications of it struck him.

It twists a man, Gordon, she had said. *It grows into something small and mean and vicious that allows him to do just what you did today with Halleck.*

Or Cheney Lee. That was his own thought. *Cheney Lee or Halleck or anybody who happened to stand in his way at the moment.* He found his anger changing to something else, a dark, frightening introspection. Was Opal right? Was he turning into that? He had not felt anything much with Tom Union, vengeance, or triumph, or anything else. He had shot the man because it had to be done; but there had been nothing personal involved. Now there was. Even with Halleck today, there was. Five years of hatred and fear and torture as a boy culminating in a vicious explosion.

He had not realized it when he was hitting Halleck, had only seen it as a natural reaction to Halleck's blocking him. Now, examining his emotions, he realized there had been a sense of triumph. Of vindication. Of revenge.

The word twisted something inside him. Was Opal right,

then? Was he heading to the other extreme? From a shy, introverted, sensitive boy—to a killer?

No!

He shook his head violently. It couldn't be. The things he had done had all been of the utmost necessity. Blackhorn had taught him that. It was a lesson he had learned the hardest way. There were times that you had to fight back. He lifted Spades to a hard gallop through town, trying to drown out the insidious doubt that filled him.

Teton Avenue became a road again, winding through the hills upon which were built the miners' shanties. Even obscured by night, there was something sordid and ugly about their haphazard squalor, strewn across the hills without any uniform pattern, following the tortured, twisted line of a lane to leave it abruptly and gather back around the mouth of an old adit. These tunnel mouths pocked the hillsides, appearing right in the center of clustered houses. At the top of the second hill, a tunnel had caved in, sucking a pair of shanties into the fall until only the beams of their roofs thrust a crazy, tilted pattern up from the hole. It brought a transitory memory of the Chinese in Bayard's office.

Then he was turning off the main road down a trail that led to the corrals and barn behind the rooming house. He unsaddled Spades and put him in a stall, and was leaving the barn when the sound came. It was a sharp, clapping explosion, from within the rooming house. Someone shouted; a window raised with a shriek. Light burgeoned into the square of another window as someone lit a lamp. Conners halted in indecision. Then thought of Blackhorn brought a sharp, sick feeling, sending him into a run toward the house.

Before he reached it, the back door smashed open and a man hit the compound, running. As he dodged between two of the miners' shanties at the foot of the hill, another man appeared in the door. He fired once at the disappearing figure.

"Blackhorn?" called Conners, still running that way.

"Get him, Gordon, get him," squalled the old man.

In automatic response, Conners wheeled toward the shacks, pulling his Remington as he ran. He ran into the narrow space between the hovels, halting in caution at the opposite end. There was furtive, running movement beyond. He raised his gun to arm's length and fired.

"My God, Harry," cried a woman from within one of the houses, "don't go out there, they'll kill you—"

There was a return shot that kicked up dirt at Conners's feet. He held his breath, every sense keyed to highest pitch, his ears filled with the mingled, undifferentiated sounds about him, picking out each one and defining it until he came to the sliding, stumbling noise of the man going up the hill between the next two houses. Knowing his quarry was running again, Conners took the chance and moved into the open.

He crossed a narrow lane to reach the next line of shacks and almost fell into one of the tunnels that had caved in right across the lane.

Then he was between two more houses. Men were calling back and forth behind him now, and someone was stirring about in this house. The flare of a match appeared weirdly through a window; it was extinguished abruptly.

"Don't show any light, you fool," he heard a man whisper hoarsely.

"But, Will," quavered a woman. "I was only—"

"Shut up. They're still out there."

Conners moved on, dodging through the houses, stopping and listening every now and then. The sounds were receding behind him now. One or two shots were apparently not enough to rouse many people in a boomtown like this. He could still hear someone's stumbling, uncertain passage ahead of him. It was receding, however, and he moved faster himself, trying to withhold his panting so he could listen. Then he went on in the utter darkness, stumbling on a rock and going to his knees. He rose and darted a few more feet, halting by an old, empty corral. It was a crazy chase, filling him with a bizarre sense of flitting, whispered, panting presence all around him. He lost the sound ahead for good, and remained crouched by another gaping adit, the ancient, rotting reek of underground depths sweeping across him as he strained his ears for some sign. For a while there was silence. Then he caught a furtive noise from behind him.

He wheeled, lifting the gun in his hand. Trapper trapped, he thought, in some vague irony. He waited, tensely, breathlessly. It came again, so soft he could not define it, yet filling his ears, in this suspended tension, like the explosion of a cannon. When it came for a third time, he could mark a definite direction. Right toward him. Right down the line of a sagging fence toward him. He cocked his gun. The sound stopped.

Again there was that painful space of waiting. He could actually hear someone breathing, in a hoarse, restrained way. He wondered if his own breathing was as audible. Clammy sweat crawled down his back. His arm began to twitch with the tension of holding out his gun.

"Somebody there?" a man asked.

Conners stiffened, realizing the voice came from behind that fence. It was such an unexpected, inane question. What the hell, he thought, let's finish it.

"Sure," he said. "It's Gordon Conners." And his index finger tensed against the trigger, ready to rake the fence with every bean in his wheel. But no shots came.

"It's MacMahon," answered the man. "I'm stableman at the rooming house. You found who shot your friend?"

"Shot?" said Conners. "Blackhorn shot?"

"You better come back," said MacMahon. "He ain't got long."

Conners headed downhill in a stumbling run, every other consideration driven from his mind. MacMahon followed him, an awkward, burly figure in the darkness, a Winchester swinging at his side. Blackhorn lay in a circle of miners and stable hands, with the rooming-house manager holding a bull's-eye lantern high for light.

The circle of saffron illumination fell across the seamed, pain-twisted face of the old man lying on a blanket spread on the ground. Gordon dropped to a knee beside him.

"Blackhorn. I didn't know you were hit. The way you came out that door—"

"Never mind. You couldn't of done anything about it. Get him?"

"No," said Conners. "Who was it?"

"I didn't see him," murmured Blackhorn. "I woke up when I heard him getting the window open from outside. I waited till he was inside and then pulled my gun from where it was lying on a chair beside the bed. He got me. . . . Get out, now, boy, for your own sake. Go as far away as you can. They'll get you sooner or later if you don't. Can't you see that? We've been crazy. They got your pa and ma, they got Willa, and now they got me. Next it'll be you, if you don't go . . ."

"Wiwilla's right here beside me, Blackhorn. It'll—"

The old man was dead. Conners stared at him, thinking how odd it was that he had seen other men die, and yet it was so different, with his pa and ma, with Wiwilla, and now with Blackhorn. He wanted to cry. He turned his face away from the closed eyes, the lifeless features. The movement took his glance across the blanket and onto the ground beside it.

There were many bootprints in the earth surrounding the blanket. Most of them were flatheeled. One set, however, were from spiked heels, leading straight to the back door of the rooming house. Everywhere they fell, they printed into the earth the clear mark of a star.

CHAPTER 10

CONNERS DID NOT feel much like riding to Harrison Basin the next day. He arranged for the funeral with the undertaker on Washakie Street. After that, there was nothing to do, and a great, somber restlessness began to fill him. He knew it was useless sitting in his room and brooding about Blackhorn. He felt responsible, somehow, for the old man's death; he should not have left him alone. Yet it did no good to think of that now.

Finally, in a bleak, bitter mood, he got Spades and headed out through Scalper Pass. He had told Bayard he would go out and look over the ranch today, and he might as well occupy himself with that, as anything.

The change in the Harrison Basin property was a shock to him. He halted his black horse at the top of the pass for ten minutes, trying to find the old sod house. He even had trouble finding where it had been. A great, gaping pit in the ground had swallowed the house, corrals, trees, everything. They had even diverted the river. And where they weren't open-pit mining, they were tunneling. The foothills eastward of where the house had stood were scarred with new adits, men and equipment moving around each tunnel mouth with the unflagging industry of ants.

Conners rode through it indifferently, a little saddened by how the mining had changed the Basin. Beyond lay the Aspens—sharp, rocky peaks tumbling into deep, cool-shadowed canyons, lush with timber and good graze. Bayard had built his home there, and it was an outfit to be proud of. The house must have cost plenty.

It was a great, colonnaded structure of many porches

and balconies, situated against the shoulder of a heavily timbered hill. French windows opened out onto a cool green lawn and a summerhouse. There were two horses at one of the tie rings before the front steps, a heavy, potent-looking piebald, stamping restlessly in the dust, and a tall chestnut with finer lines. Conners hitched his animal there and was going toward the porch when a woman called from the summerhouse. The voice was familiar, warm, motherly.

He turned and moved down a flagstone walk toward the latticed pergola. He caught sight of a mature blonde woman, and recognized her as Mrs. Bayard. A strange, small warmth filled him as he remembered that same voice, soothing him, quieting him the night of his father's death. Beyond the woman, sunlight flashed on a pair of curly, golden heads, and a child's gurgling laughter reached Conners. It had a strange effect upon him. He had seen many children in the last years, many homes. But somehow they had never touched him one way or the other. Yet that curly head, that clear, innocent laugh, the sun throwing its dappled light on the grass through the pergola—all made Conners realize, suddenly, poignantly, how long he had traveled, untied, unattached, lonely. Lonely? It made him stop, right on the walk, because he had never thought of it that way. Was it Blackhorn's death? Or seeing Opal again, after so long?

"Gordon—" Charlotte Bayard had reached him now, taking his hands, searching his face—"It's been such a long time. You've grown into such a handsome man. I'm so glad you're back, Gordon. Tell me everything that's gone on all these years."

Seeing her brought his mother back with sharp impact. He gazed into the kindly, understanding eyes, and felt a need for that understanding. He allowed her to lead him toward the summerhouse. Then all the warm, soft nostalgia faded. The lines of his face, relaxed and boyish in that instant, changed back into their habitual bleak, sharp hardness when he saw two men rise from cane chairs in the pergola, drinks in their hands. Jack Halleck and Charlie Fontenelle.

"You're a little late," said Halleck. "Roland told us you'd be out in the morning to look over the cattle setup."

There was a dark bruise mottling the flesh on the right side of his jaw. His lips lay flat against the square, chipped, chalky teeth, in a smile that was belied by the hostility of his chilly blue eyes.

"You my escort?" said Conners.

Halleck still smiled in that meaningless way. "Roland told me to be a good boy."

"Did he have to tell you?" asked Conners.

It wiped the smile off. Before Halleck could respond, Fontenelle said, "He'll be a good boy."

"Now, gentlemen," chuckled Mrs. Bayard. "It's too nice a day for this. You're setting a bad example for my children. I only let them fight on rainy days."

"Maybe it would be better if we leave, Mrs. Bayard," Conners told her. "I'm late as it is. We've got a lot to do."

"No, Gordon, you just got here—"

"He's right," said Fontenelle. "We'd better leave."

They rode deeply into the Aspens. Bayard worked none of his cattle near the house, pasturing them during spring and summer in the higher meadows of these mountains. Sometimes the trail was wide enough for the three men to ride abreast, and sometimes it narrowed to the point where they had to go single file, with Conners in the middle, and it was then that he could not help the tension that lifted his shoulders a little. Finally they came to a line camp overlooking a broad plateau covered by grazing cattle. Conners could see the white-faced Herefords, heavy and lazy among the wilder, more gaunt Texas longhorns. Conners went down among them, riding up close here or there to inspect one of the beasts.

"Your crosses don't pack as much beef as they ought to, with this kind of graze," he said.

"You can thank MacLane for that," said Fontenelle. "His boys snuck through one night and made a lot of our imported bulls into steers. The cross-breeds don't have as much whiteface in them as you'd believe from the number of Herefords we have here."

"Has MacLane got anything else in his hat besides that rustling they lynched my dad for?"

Fontenelle gave him a sharp glance. "Ain't that enough? When Bayard came back, everybody in Table Rock thought he was walking right into MacLane's lynch rope. But feeling had died down about that rustling, and Bayard had the railroad back of him. He was sitting top saddle in this section instead of MacLane. It's been war between them ever since, but Bayard is too big for MacLane to fight openly now. All he can do is bite at Bayard's heels."

"A wolf can pull down a stag twice his size doing that," Halleck said.

"A philosopher," said Fontenelle.

"You've still got some salt left in you, I see," said Conners.

"You didn't knock any out," Halleck told him. "I just wasn't expecting 'mama's boy' to come back full of vinegar. Next time I'll be ready."

"Ain't going to be no next time, Jack," Fontenelle said.

Halleck turned on him angrily, but before he could say anything, a rider showed up on the shoulder of the hill, coming from the north. His long body swayed slightly with his utter relaxation in the saddle. His face was burned to a ruddy mahogany by a lifetime of weathering, and his hooded eyes were wrinkled as an old squaw's. He drew up his horse, speaking to Fontenelle. "Crazy Moon's cut some more fence they claim crosses their pasture, and the whole bunch of them is over here going through our herd for strays. I think something's up, Charlie."

Fontenelle glanced at Conners, and Conners nodded. Without speaking, the four of them turned as one and went back the way the rider had come. They passed the line shack again, crossing a ridge. There was another stretch of open meadow beyond this. With his first sight of them, down there, it began to build in Conners. He tried to pick out MacLane from among the group of men, mounted and afoot, who were milling around. Finally he saw the man, riding a magnificent, white stallion, streaked yellow with dirt and lather.

When the Crazy Moon men became aware of the four riders led by Conners and Fontenelle, a couple of them started to lay down their wire clippers and axes, but a short word from MacLane put them back to work. Only he and another man were in the saddle to meet Conners and Bayard's men.

Conners rode down and halted his horse, then just sat there. MacLane's horse began to fiddle nervously in the abrupt silence. He jerked the beast down.

"Somebody cut out your tongue while you were away, Conners?"

Conners stared at MacLane without a word, until the silence became so unbearable even Fontenelle and Halleck began moving around nervously behind him. "Why don't you tell your men to get back on their horses and quit pretending they're working," Conners said at last.

"They won't get back on till every bit of this Buffalo Hole fence is cut down," MacLane said heavily. "It blocks access to water I've been using for ten years."

"Water that now belongs to Bayard, I take it," said Conners.

"Water that belongs to me," said MacLane. "Bayard pushed his pasture out a half mile to keep me from it."

"Can you prove that in court?"

"Not with the railroad backing Bayard," said MacLane. "You couldn't prove you existed if they didn't want you to.

I'm through trying it legally, Conners. I'm taking what belongs to me, that's all."

"You only think you are," said Conners. "Halleck, have you got a watch?"

There was no answer from behind him. He turned to see the three of them with their eyes on him. There was some affinity to the expression of their faces—the same set, dogged look that gave Conners a sinking feeling.

"I suppose you haven't got one either?" he asked Fontenelle.

"No," Fontenelle said, barely moving his lips. "I haven't got one, Conners."

Conners looked ˰t the Bayard rider. The man would not meet his eyes. h˷ knew what it was, now. They did not mean to back him. Whatever he did would be done alone. He felt his legs tighten against his horse as he turned back to MacLane.

"Maybe you've got one, then," he said.

"What for?" said MacLane, in angry surprise.

"To time you," said Conners. "I'm giving you a minute to start putting up that fence."

The muscles twitched about MacLane's mouth. Then the weight of him, shifting forward in the saddle, caused a muted creak through the whole rig. "We put a California collar on your dad, Conners. We could do the same to you."

"It's strange, MacLane," Conners told him, "that you thought you had to remind me of what you did to my father." He paused, allowing his eyes to sweep the Crazy Moon men on the ground. "That minute's started. You'd better give the order."

"I'm not giving any order except to tell them to get back to work—"

Before MacLane has finished, Conners put the spurs to his horse, and put them good. Spades bolted wildly, straight into the Crazy Moon men on the ground. The black horse's chest struck one man fully. He fell away with a hoarse cry. Another was right at Conners's stirrup, clubbing a shovel up to hit him.

Conners put his reins against the left side of Spades's neck as he leaned out to block the shovel. The animal spun on a hind heel, right into the man. It knocked him backward, and Conners tore the upraised shovel from his hands as he fell. Spinning his horse back the other way, Conners saw that MacLane had gone for his gun. But the white stallion, startled by Spades's sudden charge, had reared into the air, pedaling back into the other Crazy Moon man who was mounted; the two animals were in a squealing, fighting tangle.

This allowed Conners to turn back to the others.

One had dropped his wire clippers and pulled out his six-gun. Conners caught him on the head with his swinging shovel. He charged into another trying to run free, bringing the shovel around flat to whack him across the back and send him sprawling. Then the first shot crashed.

It came from MacLane. But his horse was still fighting, and that threw him off. Conners dropped his shovel and wheeled Spades back, drawing his Remington as he did.

He did not make the mistake MacLane had, of choosing the smaller target. He shot MacLane's horse from beneath him. Then he saw that the other rider meant to use his gun, so Conners shot his horse, twice.

MacLane pitched backward off his rearing, squealing stallion as it pawed air in the pain of its wound. Now the other animal added its wild screams to the melee, running crazily by Conners. Whatever the other men on the ground had intended, they forgot it, dropping shovels and guns as they turned to run from the crazed beast.

MacLane's stallion finished it, following the other horse, blood gushing from the wound in its chest. The white animal trampled one of the running men into the ruined fence, jumped a post they had not yet dug up, and plunged on up the slope, leaving a trail of blood in its wake.

It took Conners that long to quiet Spades and to see that none of Bayard's three men had made a move. Halleck and Fontenelle and the third rider sat their horses, holding them in tight, fiddling check against the excitement. Only Fontenelle had a gun out, an old Paterson with most of the bluing worn off, laid across his saddle horn.

MacLane rolled over onto his belly and got to his hands and knees, shaking his head.

He made a guttural sound and crawled toward the gun he had dropped a dozen feet away.

Conners found his own gun coming up and was shocked by the effort it cost him to not fire. He settled deliberately back in the saddle, trying to stifle the impulse, recognizing it for what it was. A poplar tree rose up in his mind, vivid as if it stood before him, with a man swinging from it on a rope. Then it was an elderly doctor, coming from a room, and the words were striking his head like blows. *She's just left you.*

Conners heard someone sigh deeply and realized it was himself. The sigh drew MacLane's head upward, to stare at him.

The blankness of anger in MacLane's bloodshot eyes altered to something else, a flickering of something akin to fear. Then Conners felt the stiffness of his own face, and tried to mute the taut, savage expression he knew was there.

"Go wide around that gun when you get up and start walking for home, MacLane," he said in a voice that trembled, as he lowered his own gun. "I told you, you didn't have to remind me about my dad. I won't tolerate another wrong move from you. Not the slightest one."

MacLane got up, wheezing with the effort. "You won't go free of this, Con—"

"Not a word, either, MacLane. Not one word. I think it

takes all my strength to hold this gun pointed at the ground."

Again that hunted, flickering light in the man's eyes. Watching Conners's face, with a strange, wondering expression on his own, he turned and started walking. One by one, his men had picked themselves up off the ground and turned to follow him. When they were all going, Conners turned to Fontenelle, who was still holding a gun in his hand.

"You meaning to use that on MacLane or me?"

CHAPTER 11

ALL THE WAY back to Table Rock, Conners was filled with a strange sense of frustration. He was angry at Bayard for sending him men who would not back him. And angry at himself for thinking it could be any other way. But blocking all this was another, more invidious emotion.

He could not forget his terrible desire to kill MacLane. So strong it had nauseated him; so violent it had left no room for anything else. He marveled that he had found the control to stop himself. He did not know where his restraint had come from.

Opal was right. Revenge was his motivation. His desire to help Blackhorn, to find out who had killed Wiwilla and his parents and why—all these had been minor reasons, rationalizations, hiding the real motive beneath them, so deep, so insidious, he himself had been unaware of it.

He was so preoccupied that he did not react as quickly as usual to sound. At last, however, he realized something was disturbing him, and pulled up. The faint, roaring sound of wind through the aspens. The subdued rattle of their leaves. The chatter of a chipmunk, an isolated sound. When it ceased abruptly, he understood what was wrong. There were no other small animal sounds. Close to him, that could be understandable. But ahead of him, far enough away so his presence had not yet reached them, they were still silent. He pulled Spades off the road into the cover of timber.

For a while the silence continued. Then, softly, he began to get it. A faint, strange crackling.

A horse moving on the pine needles above this belt of

aspens. Realizing it might be a long shot, he pulled the old Joslyn-Tomes from under his stirrup leather and slipped a shell softly into the breech. He had another wait, until the man appeared, coming down through the aspens from above, fifty yards ahead of Conners, peering up and down the road in a puzzled way.

"Looking for me, Simms?"

Sheriff Murphy Simms stiffened in the saddle, whirling to stare at Conners. Then he settled back, a relieved expression softening his face, and turned his pony toward Conners. He was a tall, dour man, sloppily dressed in old cavalry trousers; a fleece-lined canvas mackinaw obscured the gaunt lines of his torso, winter or summer. As inevitable as the mackinaw was the cold butt of a big black cigar held between his tobacco-stained teeth. He removed this, and spat.

"You see me?"

"Heard you."

Simms put the stogie back in, cocking his head to squint at Conners. "Damn it, Gordon, I heard you had ears like that, but I never believed it. Say you can move uncommonly fast, too." He took out the stogie once more, chose a spot on the ground with great care, and spat. "I wanted to talk with you about your partner's death."

"Why didn't you just come up and ask?"

"There was somebody else riding herd on you. I wanted to wait and see what developed."

"Somebody else? Who?"

"I didn't get a look. He seemed to be following you from Harrison Basin. Maybe he saw me and spooked."

Conners nodded, unsmiling. "So—what do you want to know about Blackhorn's death?"

"Going back to town?" asked Simms.

"I was."

"I'll ride along."

Conners glanced at him, stuffed the rifle back in its

sheath, and turned Spades down onto the road. Simms followed, his unkempt little pony so short the rider's legs almost scraped ground. He smiled vaguely at Conners. "You hold it against me that I didn't show up and stop your pa's lynching, don't you, son?"

"Isn't that a natural reaction?"

"Damn natural. Only look at it from my saddle. A man's got to use his head in my spot, Gordon, or lose it. Examine the facts closely and ask yourself, in all truth, if I could have stopped that crew from stringing up your dad."

Conners stared at the black, twitching ears of his horse. "I suppose you're right, Simms. No one man could."

"In fact, anyone who tried was just as liable to get hung as your pa. Isn't that so?"

"I guess feeling was pretty high."

"Clear the slate a little?"

Conners drew a heavy breath, looking off impatiently to the side. "Okay, Simms. Okay."

Simms rode silently for a space, studying the trees. "This Blackhorn and your father worked together on the railroad, didn't they? Mixed up in the Arapahoe Wells affair."

"You seem to know."

"Never did catch the man who killed the paymaster."

"That's right."

"Is that who cut a notch for Blackhorn yesterday?"

Conners looked at him narrowly. "You still seem to know."

"I never did think your dad rustled those cattle," said Simms. "And now you're marked down, is that it? That must be a mighty uncomfortable feeling. Especially when you're all alone." He pursed his lips, rolling the stogie into the other side of his mouth. "You wouldn't need to be alone, Gordon."

Conners studied him again. "I can't believe your interest is entirely unselfish."

"It's selfish as hell," said Simms. "I knuckled under to

MacLane for a long time, Gordon. I kept from going out
and trying to stop them from lynching your father. I did
a lot of other scurvy, yellow little things, till I couldn't
stand the taste in my mouth anymore. And then I backed
him and got squeezed out for it." He wheeled to Conners,
frowning. "Tell me the truth, Gordon. Is MacLane the
one?"

Conners shook his head. "I don't know. Neither did Pa
nor Blackhorn. The holdup man wasn't seen by any of
them that night, though he must have thought they saw
him, and that's why he's tried to get rid of them."

"Do you *think* it's MacLane, then?"

"How do I know?" said Gordon.

"He's a likely candidate, isn't he?"

"I've thought of him. But he never worked for the
railroad."

"I've looked into his past," said Simms. "He was trailing
cattle up about that time. He went broke in Cheyenne
before the railroad was there."

Conners could not help smiling wryly at the man. "If it
is him, and you flushed him, you'd have a good crack at
office next election, wouldn't you?"

"I told you it wasn't an unselfish motive. I want to be
sheriff again. I was in that office so long I can't do
anything else. There were twenty thousand dollars of
securities stolen in that Arapahoe Wells holdup, you know.
Negotiable securities that haven't showed up yet. If someone uncovered them for the Union Pacific, he'd be the
fair-haired boy around here. That isn't the only bird this
stone would kill. The pressure on that sheriff's office
makes it hell for a man who considers himself halfway
decent. If MacLane was in on the Arapahoe Wells affair,
and we could prove it, a lot of that pressure would be
removed. How about it?"

"There's one way I can see of skylighting the man who

shot Blackhorn in a hurry," said Conners. "He still wants me, so he must be around. That would call for a decoy."

"Who?"

"Me."

Connors had a bandage on his right hand when he saw Bayard the next morning. Bayard was sympathetic, and Conners told him in a sullen way that one of the Crazy Moon men had broken it with a shovel in the fight. Then he let Bayard know he was mad, and let him know he was going back to Harrison Basin alone this afternoon to do the job his way, and Bayard could keep his muscle men here. Bayard tried to placate him, telling him he was free to take care of the cattle any way he chose, just so he halted the trouble MacLane was causing.

After this, Conners went down to eat lunch, then idled around town, acquainting himself with half a dozen of the biggest, most-frequented saloons. There were men he knew in most of them, and though he did not talk loudly, they found out how he had broken his hand. He did not get obviously drunk, but when he left town in the afternoon, he was sitting Spades in a casual, swaying way, with a meaningless grin on his face.

The aspens were browning with summer, and the water was drying up in the creek that paralleled the road into Scalper Pass. His black horse stirred the thick tawny dust until it hung like a ragged pennant for ten yards behind, settling smokily into the road again. An oriole was warbling down in the bottoms, and a woodpecker kept up an intermittent tattoo.

It was near evening by the time he reached the middle of the pass, with the sunlight coming through the trees in long, bronze shafts, his figure fluttering through these like a shadow moving down a picket fence. He had been trying to retain that relaxed, inebriated seat in the saddle, but when the oriole stopped singing behind him, he felt tension tighten the little muscles in his face, his neck, his back.

He moved the bandaged hand till it was in plain sight. The woodpecker started up again, then halted sharply. There was no sound, now, save the muffled plod of Spades's hooves in summer dust.

"All right, Conners!"

The voice came from up on the slope, in a loud, hoarse shout. Conners took a dive off one side of his horse. The shot came as he struck the ground, whining across Spades's saddle to bite out a chunk of dirt twenty feet beyond where Conners was rolling across the earth. Any good rider could fall that way, and roll onto his feet. He had not yet gained them, however, with Spades squealing and galloping off down the road behind him, when more gunfire came from up on the slope, along with Simms's voice again.

"Look out, Conners, he's coming back that way—"

Conners was just coming to his feet when the piebald burst into the open, with its rider halfway off the other side to avoid being knocked down by a branch. That was why Conners could not recognize him. Still in that position, the man began firing wildly.

I ain't going to have no fancy gunman in my string, boy. If you're shooting from the hip, it means you're in a hurry, and if you're in a hurry, you're spooked.

Blackhorn's words filled Conners's mind. It all happened in an instant, but it seemed like a long unhurried space. With the rider's wild bullets knocking bark off the trees and kicking dirt up from the ground, Conners held his gun out at arm's length, and when the man's swaying, jerking body swung up on the horse, righting itself, Conners fired.

The rider pitched backward off his horse as it bolted, flopped over a couple of times, and came to rest in the middle of the road, dust settling slowly back about his body. By the time Simms came riding down out of the trees, Conners was beside the dead man, looking at the star imprinted in the heel of each boot.

"That the one?" asked Simms.

"That's the one," said Conners. "I didn't want it to happen this way. It isn't at all the way it should have happened. I needed to talk with him. This doesn't resolve anything."

Simms got down off his horse, slipping a toe under the dead man's arm to roll him over. His face turned blank with surprise.

"That's Charlie Fontenelle!"

CHAPTER 12

A STRANGE, GARBLED sound was rising from Table Rock, discernible to Conners and Simms long before they reached the end of Scalper Pass and came to the junction of Teton Avenue and Harrison Basin Road. Here they could look down into Chinatown and see that Peking Alley was a shambles.

Apparently one of the old mining shafts had collapsed, swallowing a dozen joss houses and flimsy shanties on one side of the street. A fire had started on that side, spreading to the other, gutting the buildings there. Long lines of a bucket brigade spread from the burning structures, and they seemed to have it under control. Under the fading billows of black smoke, however, a seething, muttering crowd stirred, moving restlessly up and down Shanfoo Street, and the other alleys and narrow avenues of the section. It seemed to have its center at the larger joss houses on the corner of Shanfoo and Teton, where someone on a balcony was exhorting the mob. Conners saw that it was Cheney Lee.

Lee's voice carried to them over the muttering and the sporadic shouts of the crowd. There was something hoarsely fanatical to it. He was speaking Chinese, and though it was unintelligible to Conners, Simms pulled up, frowning.

"What is it?" Conners said. "You speak Chinese?"

"A little. I used to handle a work gang on the railroad," said Simms. He tilted his head, trying to make out the words. "*Yua tsu'i.* That's guilty. *Faat kwok.* That has something to do with French."

"Bayard?" asked Conners.

Simms's head jerked to him. "Yeah." He nodded, trying to hear again. *"Li Bye yet kit.* That's Monday.

"That's it. He's telling them Bayard is to blame for this. *Nga moon.* That's court of justice. No court of justice. They've suffered all these years and it's time somebody paid. He's sending them up to Bayard, Conners. I've never seen anything like this before. I've never seen them fight back like this in my life. Let's get around to Gammon. . . ."

They could not have forced their way up Teton, but Gammon was a block over, running parallel with the main avenue. This was predominantly white, with little knots of miners and townspeople shifting around indecisively, gathering on corners and milling across the street, calling back and forth to each other.

"What's up, Harry?"

"I don't know. The Chinamen are up to something."

"Where's the sheriff, Walt?"

"Somebody said he's down at Cheyenne on a case. We ought to do something. They're marching up Teton Avenue."

"Get that started and we'll have a race war on our hands," muttered Simms, kneeling his pony through a thin scattering of men. They reached Fourth and turned back toward Teton. From here they could see that the Union Pacific building was surrounded. Most of the shouting, pulling, shifting crowd were Chinese, but Conners caught sight of more than one white miner in the middle. Then something cold touched him. A rope had appeared above the crowd, knotted into a hangnoose. At this moment, a woman came running through the knots of onlookers at this end of Fourth. Her bonnet was torn off as she forced herself through, but she kept on coming toward Conners. It was Opal Hamilton.

"Gordon," she cried breathlessly, her face twisted in horror. "It's a lynch mob. A dozen families were caught in the cave-in down on Peking Alley, and half of them are dead. They're holding Bayard responsible, and they're going to lynch him. You've got to do something, Gordon."

"Lynch him?" Conners stared up at the building, a strange quietude filling him after all the excited tension of the last moment. He felt his lips twist, and did not know it was a bleak, humorless smile, till he saw the horror in Opal's face.

"What is it?" she said.

"I was just thinking how ironic it would be if Bayard were lynched, too."

"What do you mean, *too*?"

His saddle creaked as he bent toward her. "We've just been out on Scalper Pass, Opal, setting a trap for the man who had been following Blackhorn and me for so long."

"The one with stars on his boots?" she said, and then her eyes were caught on his unbandaged right hand. "It wasn't really broken, then?"

"No. But everybody in town thought it was. I figured he'd find out—either see me, or get word—and think I'd be in Scalper Pass alone, drunk, with a hand I couldn't use to shoot with. Simms followed along the ridge and tipped me off."

"Gordon, you might have been killed—" she broke off, staring at him, and then asked it in a hushed, reluctant way. "Who was it?"

"Charlie Fontenelle."

Her chest rose sharply with her indrawn breath. Then, automatically, she looked over her shoulder at the U. P. building, at the windows of Roland Bayard's offices on the third floor. When she turned back, her eyes were wide.

"You're not saying . . . that Bayard . . . ?"

"What else?" said Conners. "Fontenelle worked for Bayard, didn't he?"

"But why—?"

"A lot of reasons," said Conners. "The coal on the Harrison Basin property, for instance. Fontenelle went clear up in the Wind Rivers after me, didn't he? Bayard wanted me out of the way bad. As bad as he wanted Dad out of the way when he found out there was coal on that land."

"That's just guessing."

"It's facts," said Conners. "Bayard wouldn't show me the books when I came back. He's been stalling me off ever since I first saw him at his office. He sent me out to fight MacLane with a crew that wouldn't back me up. If Mac-Lane had killed me, that would have been all right, too, wouldn't it?"

She shook her head from side to side. "No, Conners, I can't believe it's Bayard—"

"Then take a look at this," he said, pulling a charred, torn piece of paper from his pocket and handing it to Opal. "We found it on Charlie Fontenelle. It's one of the negotiable securities that was stolen from the train along with the payroll at Arapahoe Wells."

A pale, pinched look entered her face as she stared at it. "You think this means Charlie Fontenelle held up the train?"

"No," said Conners. "Blackhorn never did think the man with the star on his boots was the man who did the job at Arapahoe Wells. He was only hired by the real holdup man. Fontenelle had to be away long periods of time when he was on our trail. If he was working for Bayard, he couldn't have done it without Bayard's knowledge. Or Bayard's orders."

She looked again at the office, then turned back to Conners. "So you've condemned Bayard," she said in a hollow voice.

"He's condemned himself."

"And you're going to let them hang him."

"Don't you believe in poetic justice?" Conners asked.

"You're mocking it," she said. "They're going to kill a man, and you're mocking it. If Bayard was the one who held up the train, why should Fontenelle be carrying this torn piece of security around, knowing it would damn him if he were found with it?"

"There are a lot of little pieces that will probably never be known," said Simms. "The main facts are there. Even I have to admit it, Miss Hamilton. I had MacLane pegged all along as the one behind this. But I've seen courts of law convict a man on much less evidence than this."

"How do you know they'd do it here?" Opal said hotly. "Would the evidence that hanged your dad have stood up in a court of law, Gordon? All those hotheaded fools had was one fact. They didn't have the whole story at all. The whole story came out afterward, and half the people in town realized your father had been framed. All you have here is one side of the story."

"More than one side, Opal. A dozen sides that all fit in."

She bit her lip, looking away in a thoughtful way as if seeking something to convince him. "I understand you saw Mrs. Bayard the other day."

He frowned at this irrelevancy. "Yes."

"Lovely woman, isn't she?" Opal's voice was thin.

"I always did like Mrs. Bayard."

"Beautiful kids, too. What do you think it will do to them? Do you think it will twist their lives as much as it has yours? Do you think it will cause Mrs. Bayard as much grief as it did your mother—so much grief she dies from it?"

"My mother was shot!"

"The doctor told us she could have lived if she'd wanted to," said Opal. "She knew her man was dead and she didn't have the will to fight. Maybe Mrs. Bayard won't even have to be shot. She worships Roland. And what if they find out he was innocent after it's all over? Where will that leave you?"

"What could Gordon do anyway, Miss Hamilton?" asked

Simms. "That crowd's in a frenzy. Gordon would get killed himself if he tried to stop it now."

Opal was staring at Conners. "I told you it wasn't what you did before. It was how you felt about it. If you let them do this now, it's because you think Bayard is guilty. You think there's justice in it, and you're condemning him without even giving him a chance to talk."

"He didn't give my dad a chance to talk," said Conners. "Or my mother. Or Wiwilla. Maybe it's lucky Bayard can't talk. I'd keep seeing my young wife, or that old man dying in the yard of a miners' rooming house down near Peking Alley. I'd keep seeing my dad swinging from that tree—"

"You're going to let them hang a man who may be utterly innocent of the crimes he's accused of!"

Opal turned on the last word, heading back toward the mob. Conners tried to hold down the smoldering, righteous hatred of Bayard he had first felt with the discovery of Charlie Fontenelle. There was no reason why he should risk his life, probably lose it, in a futile attempt to save the man who had killed the four people closest to him in his life.

But somehow, that hate, that anger began to dissipate in the face of his doubts. Did Fontenelle's actions really prove that Bayard was guilty? Was Opal right? She was about his father. The men who had hanged him had been led into it by evidence that gave a wrong picture.

The noise of the crowd was growing. More ropes were in evidence. The crowd itself was growing, spilling back this way down Fourth Street until it lapped at the doorway in which Opal now stood. The sounds were wilder, more frightening. The terror it could instill made him think of his own terror that night, running with his wounded mother from a kill-crazy hang-mob. His mother? . . . Mrs. Bayard. It was a logical sequence, and it brought him to the thought of those curly-headed kids in the summer-house.

He seemed to twitch under a stab of guilt. He shook his head savagely. That wasn't right. It was Bayard who was guilty. And yet, if he let a man die who wasn't guilty . . . Again he saw Mrs. Bayard's face, mingled with his mother's now, stirring in restless pain beneath a blanket.

Conners's black horse fiddled nervously beneath him. Staring at the crowd, he spoke in a tight-lipped, reluctant way. "Simms, do you think Bayard is guilty?"

"I've seen a jury hang a man on less evidence," said Simms. Then he peered sharply at Conners. "You ain't getting any crazy notions in your mind? Don't listen to that woman, Conners. Even if he was innocent, you couldn't help him now."

"That's it," said Conners. "There's even a doubt in your mind."

"No. Don't be a fool, Conners."

"Do you still want that sheriff's job back, Simms?"

"Sure, but I—"

"Then here's your chance to prove it."

The U. P. roundhouse and yards were down at Seventh and Gammon, and Simms rode with Conners, cursing all the way. In the warehouse was stored the equipment for the maintenance crews. Conners found an old man on duty. He had to argue to get what he wanted but when the old man found out what it was for, he gave in. Conners rode carefully back down Gammon to Fourth, the box cradled delicately in both arms, with Simms trailing at a short distance. They turned down Fourth again. The crowd filled a greater length of the street now, only a hundred yards of it left toward Gammon. Simms dismounted and took the box from Conners. Then Conners stepped off.

They had pried up the top of the box at the warehouse, and all Conners had to do was rip off the slate now. He picked out one of the long, sinister cylinders.

"Most of those Chinese have worked on the railroad or in the mines, haven't they?" he said.

"Probably not a one among them who hasn't."

"Then I guess they'll know what dynamite is." Conners lit the strip of fuse the old man had given them. "You pick up the box," he told Simms. "I'll carry one stick in my hand, the fuse in the other. I'll tell you what to say to them when we get near enough."

A Chinese man in a black silk jacket and wooden shoes on the fringe of the crowd was first to see them. He held a long staff in his hand, shaking it at the building, and he turned to stare at what Conners had. Conners had never seen so much expression in an Oriental face before. He began squealing something in his own language and tearing at the man next to him. In a moment, a dozen of them were looking toward Conners.

"Now," Conners told Simms. "Tell them to break it up. Tell them if they don't scatter and get back to Chinatown, I'm starting to throw these things."

Simms began, in a halting, broken way, searching for the words. What he said was repeated back into the press. Conners heard the same words over and over, in high, singsong voices. When he thought enough of them understood, he moved the burning fuse a little nearer the stick of dynamite he held. It caused a violent stir in the crowd, the ranks nearest him breaking backward and away to either side. He kept walking forward, inexorably, implacably, holding his face carefully expressionless. Then somebody began to shout from across Teton Avenue.

"Conners, you fool, get out of here with that. You'll be killed. They'll tear you to bits. You're saving a criminal. Bayard is responsible for the death of over a dozen people in that cave-in—"

"It's Cheney Lee on the balcony of the Teton House," said Simms. "How'd he get up there?"

"Probably up Washakie Street and in the back way,"

Conners muttered. Then he raised his voice to Lee. "Tell your people to break it up, Lee. If you incite them any further a lot of people besides Bayard will suffer. The Americans down on Gammon Street are gathering up a party with guns. If you don't get these Chinese out of here, you'll have a war on your hands."

"A war we will win," screamed Lee. "Long enough have we suffered under your oppression. Long enough have we been lynched and beaten and used by you. No more will it be a Chinese hanging from some tree by his neck because he happened to walk on the wrong side of the street, or lying shot to death in the gutter at the whim of some drunken teamster. My people are aroused now, Conners, and nothing will stop them—"

He trailed off into Chinese, turning to shout at the mob, a tall, wild, frightening figure on the balcony, black hair down about his face, eyes flashing white against the dark, raw planes of his Mongoloid cheekbones.

"He's telling them to get you," said Simms. "Back out, now, Gordon, while you still can."

"I'm going on ahead, Simms," said Conners, walking steadily forward. "If you want to leave, I won't blame you."

"Oh, why in hell did I ever want to be sheriff again?" moaned Simms.

Conners went on forward, and Simms continued beside him. There was an uncertain, eddying surge along the foremost ranks, in response to Cheney Lee's wild, pealing shouts. Conners felt his whole body draw up.

"They're going to do it," cried Simms. "He's got a grip on them, Conners. You'll have to use these things."

"Have I got enough room between us to drop one without hurting anybody?" shouted Conners, above the rising din.

"Do it before they break," Simms yelled. "You've only got another second. If they break and start running, you'll blow some of them up sure as Shanghai—"

Conners touched the fuse to the stick he held and, praying that he had gauged the distance right, tossed it. The stick landed exactly halfway between the two men and the crowd. The foremost ranks had been surging and eddying forward, on the point of breaking and running for Conners. Now a wild, fearful shout went up, and they threw themselves back on the crowd. Conners and Simms went to the ground, Simms spinning around to put his body between the box of dynamite and the explosion.

Then it came. The earth trembled beneath him, and his head rang. A great, billowing cloud of smoke and earth was thrown into the air, clods and rocks and chunks of hard ground pelted back down, forming a sullen, shuddering tattoo against Conners's head and shoulders. Before this had ceased, he was back on his feet, snatching another stick of dynamite from the box in Simms's hands.

Now, through the settling dust and debris, he could see a dozen Chinese strewn on the ground before the bulk of the crowd, and three or four times that number thrown back against the mob by the force of the explosion, on their knees against the press, or draped around a fellow countryman. One by one, the Chinese on the ground were rising and stumbling fearfully toward the bulk of their people, until they were all up, and Conners could see that none of them was actually hurt.

"That did it," said Simms, rising to his feet. "The whole mob knows what's up on this side now."

Conners moved on forward, the sweat drenching him, the second stick of dynamite held high with the fuse. Cheney Lee was shouting again from the balcony, but he could not halt the movement of the crowd, slow at first, impeded by its very size, gathering momentum, back down Teton Avenue toward Chinatown. Conners caught sight of a gun flashing above the dark, swaying silhouette of heads and conical hats.

"Tell them if they shoot me I can still throw a couple of

these things before I go down," Conners called to Simms. "Tell them what the odds are against killing me with the first shot, and how much chance there is I'll be able to blow up a couple of dozen of them before they can finish me."

Again Simms called, his tense, searching voice rising above the other mingled sounds. And they kept moving forward, forcing the crowd farther and farther back, until Conners and Simms were at the intersection, with the other side of the mob beginning to break up and scatter before the pressure of those behind them. Conners was in a position where he could see up into the open windows of Bayard's office now, and recognize Bayard standing in the opening.

"I can't tote this box another step, Conners," moaned Simms.

"I don't think you'll have to," said Conners. "They're going now."

He glanced up at the Teton Hotel. Cheney Lee was no longer there. The U. P. men and townspeople streamed from the bank and doorways all up and down the street to gather around Conners and Simms, clapping them on the back and offering them drinks, filling the street with an excited babble. Conners worked his way through it toward the U. P. building. A hand caught him in the vestibule, pulling him into an open door of an empty office. It was Opal Hamilton, face flushed and shining, a wondering look in her eyes.

"I didn't think you'd do it. When I left you, I thought it was the last time I'd want to see you. You don't know what it did to me, Gordon." She searched his face. "You still think Bayard is guilty of your father's death?"

"I can't see it any other way. But you were right," he said. "Is that what you want me to say?"

"If it's the truth."

"It is. You were right. I tried to tell myself I came back

to claim my inheritance to help Blackhorn, even because of Wiwilla. But when it came right down to it, when I was brought up against my past—Halleck, MacLane, Bayard, the whole ugly thing—revenge blotted out all those other motives."

"And then—"

"Mrs. Bayard, I guess. Those kids. I couldn't cause them the grief it had caused my mother. If there was a chance that Bayard was innocent, I had to give him that chance."

She was up against him, breathing deep. "Do you remember that night we were talking about what you had been as a boy? You said it was only part of you. I told you I couldn't see it at all anymore."

"I remember."

"I see it now, Gordon. Those callouses have worn off. You can feel the things you used to. You've had to go from one extreme to the other to find out where a man should stand, but now you know. You're not a coward. You're not a killer. You're a man, Gordon. You may think you grew up a long time ago, but today is the first time you really earned the right to be called a man."

"Opal, I was a man the night I married Wiwilla."

She caught his hand. "You're not going up to Bayard, now?"

"I am," he said. "I'm not going to let him know what we suspect him of, but I'd like to see him."

Her voice lifted in some small fear. "Gordon—"

He smiled crookedly at her. "Just remember, Opal, it was your man who incited that mob."

CHAPTER 13

BAYARD's OFFICE WAS full of excited, gesticulating men, but as soon as Conners entered the room, Bayard jumped from his chair behind the desk and grabbed his arm, pumping his hand.

"Gordon, I wish there were some way to thank you. I never saw anything like it. I thought I was done for sure. They had the place surrounded. And with that yellow-livered sheriff running the minute he heard there was a mob gathering—"

"Maybe you need a new sheriff." Conners smiled faintly, tilting his head toward Simms, who had come up with him.

Bayard looked at Simms in some surprise. Then he threw back his head, laughing loudly. "By heck, maybe we do. I'll take it up with the council the first thing tomorrow morning. And now come into the other room, Gordon, and I'll show you what a quarter of a million dollars looks like."

Conners's face went blank with surprise. Then he followed Bayard into the other room.

Bayard introduced a tall, thin, gray-headed man as Carterwright, a U. P. bookkeeper.

"He just brought the books back from Cheyenne today, Gordon. Show him how it works, Carterwright."

The man turned to a high desk covered with ledgers. It took him a few minutes to show Conners how they were kept. Everything was listed under Conners-Bayard. The coal revenue wasn't the only income listed. There were profits off the cattle, investments in U. P. stocks, real estate within Table Rock, a silver-mining development up in the Owl Creeks.

"I don't quite understand it, Roland," said Conners. "You have the profits on your cattle ranch listed under the company name. And these investments on U. P. preferred were taken from your half of the coal revenues."

Bayard came over to put his arm around Conners's shoulders. "We're partners, aren't we, Gordon? Don't partners always split the profits?"

"But you wouldn't have had to split the dividends on those stocks. The original investment could have been made with your own money. And the cattle development is yours."

"It would have been taking advantage of you while you were away," said Bayard. "I knew if you were here, you'd want to invest some of that coal money."

"If partners split the profits, they also split the losses," said Conners. "How about this loss you took on the mining development last year? You've got it listed under your coal revenue."

Bayard shrugged, grinning. "I wouldn't want you to think I was investing your money in a losing proposition."

Conners turned to him, unwilling to believe it. "In other words, when we made money, half of it was mine. When we lost it, the burden was completely on your shoulders."

Bayard stirred uncomfortably. "I felt sort of like a guardian to you, Gordon, what with your father and me having been so close."

Conners shook his head dazedly. "How about the property on Peking Alley, Roland? I don't see that listed anywhere."

"We don't own that, Gordon," said Bayard. "I tried to tell Cheney Lee that the other day. The railroad used to own that block as company houses. But they condemned them two years ago. Somebody bought them up at that time, but those fool Chinamen still have it in their minds that the railroad owns them."

Conners stared at Bayard a long time, feeling sick, somehow. Then he went over to a chair, seating himself, head in his hands.

"What's the matter, Gordon?" asked Bayard.

Conners lifted his head to stare at Simms. "What do you think?"

"The same thing you're thinking," said Simms.

Conners turned to Bayard. "Roland, I think I've done you an awful injustice."

He told them, then, the whole thing. Bayard's face turned pale.

He walked to the window, staring out, running his hand through rumpled hair.

"And you thought I'd sent Fontenelle out to kill you?" he said. He shook his head from side to side, turning back. "Fontenelle had only worked for me about six months. During that time he'd given me no cause to suspect anything like this. You were justified in coming to the conclusion you did, Gordon. I just can't understand you thinking that, and still doing what you did today."

Conners showed Bayard the security. "It's the one from the Arapahoe Wells holdup, all right," Bayard told them. "I knew your father's brother was sent up for it, but I never suspected your father was working to free him that way. You say whoever did that holdup had made several attempts on your father's life before?"

"Yes," said Gordon. "Though I didn't know it till I met Blackhorn. Simms was surprised when the man with stars in his boots turned out to be working for you. He'd had his eye on MacLane from the beginning."

"And this brings us right back to him," said Simms.

"Wasn't MacLane in Cheyenne about the time of the Arapahoe Wells affair?" Bayard asked Carterwright.

The bookkeeper nodded. "I was working for the U. P.

there. MacLane came in with a Texas trail herd. They all had Texas fever and nobody would buy them. It broke him. The holdup happened very shortly afterward."

"And MacLane bought his Crazy Moon up here about a month later," said Bayard.

"Good arithmetic," Simms murmured.

Bayard looked at the security again. "This is the first one of these I've ever seen. Whoever got them off that pay train has been holding onto them."

"For a rainy day, maybe?" said Simms.

"It would have been dangerous to try and pass them very soon after the crime," said Bayard. He ran a hand speculatively through his disheveled hair. "But now, say the man is forced to the wall, and has no other way to raise the cash, and will lose what holdings he has unless he does raise the cash. Don't you figure he'd think enough time had passed so he could safely dump the securities?"

Conners saw the direction of his thought. "Could MacLane be forced to the wall?"

"He's already pretty close to it," said Bayard. "That bad winter last year wiped out most of his beef. He's mortgaged to the hilt. Isn't that what you were telling me, Carterwright?"

The bookkeeper nodded. "I know the P. A. who handles his books. He says the only thing that's keeping MacLane above water is that contract he's got with Pacific Northern to supply them with beef for their labor gangs on the spur they're building through the Owl Creeks."

"Isn't Pacific Northern a subsidiary of U. P.?" asked Conners.

"U. P. owns controlling stock," Bayard said, nodding. "If you mean we could bring pressure to bear and have the contract canceled, that's an idea. Old man Hayden owns MacLane's first mortgage and he'd foreclose soon enough if MacLane couldn't meet the payment."

"Then the problem would be where MacLane would try

to dump those securities," said Simms. "Isn't his cousin assistant manager of the Table Rock bank?"

"Edgar Malloy," Bayard said. "It's likely MacLane would try to channel them through him. But we can't go to Malloy—he's too thick with MacLane."

"There's a chief teller in the bank who worked with me on several cases while I was sheriff," said Simms. "I think he'd come through for us."

Bayard's vivid eyes began to flash with excitement. "It looks like the setup, then. How about it, Conners? The man with those securities is the man who's made this unholy mess of your life. Shall we put the squeeze on MacLane and see what comes out?"

"Yes," said Conners, staring at him. "Let's see."

It was long waiting after that. Bayard pulled the strings to have MacLane's contract canceled with Pacific Northern. MacLane was in town that weekend visiting cattle buyers and left in obvious anger. Conners himself checked on the buyers, purportedly to try and dump some of Bayard's stock. It was a low market and none of them would bid. In the course of conversation he found out from most of them that they had not bought from MacLane either. Then old man Hayden came in from his home outside town, visiting only one place, his lawyer's office. Conners began to feel the excitement of it as the pattern took definite form.

The teller in the Table Rock National, Bill Crane, was a tall, sharp-faced man, with keen, incisive eyes behind spectacles. He met with Simms and Conners; Simms had already explained the situation to him. Crane told them the securities would not necessarily come through him, but if a bank draft was drawn in payment, or any cash was used, he could find out about it.

They arranged for him to keep in constant touch with Simms. The men's room in the bank faced out across

Teton to the Teton Hotel. It had two high windows with pull shades. The teller was to pull the right one up and down three times if he wanted to see Simms. Simms rented a room in the Teton overlooking the street, and the two men started spending the bulk of their days there.

The signal came three days after old man Hayden had showed up in town. It was about four o'clock, and Conners was at the window while Simms was catching some sleep in the bed. Conners woke Simms and told him the shade had been pulled.

They met Crane in an eating place half a block down Teton, taking a booth. The man was excited.

"It came this afternoon. About ten minutes ago. I was working after hours. Malloy didn't know I was in the bank. He came out of his office and went for the safe before he saw me. There was a sheaf of those securities on his desk. I could see it through his open door. There was a man in there too. You know that dope addict they call Faro."

"I saw him with MacLane the first day I was here," said Conners.

"When he gets the money, he'll probably leave by the side door onto the alley," said Crane.

He did. They waited in the bar opposite the alley. The man came out the side door in a few minutes, long tailcoat flapping about his legs, and turned down toward Gammon. Both Simms and Conners got their horses. They couldn't follow him through the alley without being seen, so Simms raced down Fourth toward Gammon, while Conners took Spades down Teton to Third, then down Third to Gammon. He had hardly reached Gammon before he saw Faro on the sidewalk, coming toward him from the alley. Conners pulled back behind a string of Murphy wagons and watched the man cross Third, going on down Gammon.

He waited till Simms reached the corner, then gave the man his horse and told him to follow about a half a block behind, while he, on foot, could keep closer to Faro without being spotted. They crossed Second, and then First, on Gammon. Conners kept waiting for the man to reach a horse. But Faro kept walking. This was Chinatown, now. The peeling gilt of signs was giving way to the red-and-black ideograph posters plastered on flimsy walls and storefronts. Men in silk coats and sandals stood in little knots in the doorways and on the curbs. Conners could feel the hostility of their eyes on him. Then it was Peking Alley, running parallel to First.

Faro turned, passing down Peking Alley to Teton. The crowds thickened here. They were celebrating again, with that huge bizarre dragon, carried by thirty or forty men, winding through the streets and alleys to make obeisance before business houses.

Peking Alley ended abruptly. It had extended further, but the houses and buildings beyond, where the alley had wound up the hill, were now nothing but a pile of rubble sucked down by the cave-in of the old mine tunnel. Faro turned into the doorway of the last building in the line of those still standing. He glanced back, and Conners shifted behind a group of Chinese. Then Faro disappeared, and Conners hurried down toward the door.

A group of young men started gathering in the opening to block his way. Conners did not mean to be stopped. He kept right on going, shouldering into their press. They began shouting and pushing at him. He caught an arm and swung the man back out, sunk his free fist into another one's belly. It gave him a hole and he plunged through. The door was unlocked, opening into a small entrance hall.

The luxuriance of the interior, after the shabby dilapidation on the outside, astounded him. Aubusson, with inch-deep nap, carpeted the floors. Tables of teak and ivory stood beneath an ornate mirror crusted with gold filigree. He heard voices down the hall and walked on. He came to a closed door. Tried the knob. Locked.

He fired twice at the lock, then kicked the door open. The room was smoky with incense. There was a huge teak desk, before which stood Faro in his moth-eaten frock coat; he turned toward Conners in twitching, disorganized surprise. Behind the desk stood Cheney Lee.

CHAPTER 14

CONNERS STARED AT Cheney Lee for a long silent moment, then at the money in his hands. "I guess I should have waited for you to take it to MacLane," he said at last.

It had taken this long for the surprised anger to recede from Cheney Lee's face. His smile seemed to cause him an effort.

"Or maybe if MacLane had gotten it, he would have brought it to you," said Conners.

"Your mind jumps around like a monkey, Mr. Conners."

"The U. P. had Chinese labor when they were putting that track across Nebraska and Wyoming, didn't they," said Conners. It was coming together in his mind with surprising lucidity, after the first shock of finding this man instead of MacLane. "Maybe you were on one of those gangs."

"What a loathsome thought," said Lee.

Conners said, "That's just about it. Loathsome enough to make you hold up the pay train? My uncle chased you and you shot him and stuck some of the money in his hand to transfer suspicion. Only, by the time you did that, my dad and Blackhorn were coming up, and you thought they had seen you. That's why you were trying to get rid of them all these years. You were the one who had those rustled Crazy Moon cows put in our pasture, knowing how bitter feeling was. You were the one who had Tom Union and Charlie Fontenelle following me."

"Guessing is a poor substitution for facts," said Lee.

"Then give me the facts."

"If you will drop the gun."

"Don't be a fool."

"I might ask the same of you. Press the knife a little deeper, Chang. He does not seem to feel it."

Conners stiffened, the point of the knife biting through his coat into the flesh of his back. Slowly, reluctantly, he opened his fingers. The Remington hit the floor with a heavy thud. There was no effort to Lee's smile now; it held a veiled, ironic triumph. He came around the desk.

"Perhaps it went a little further than the personal shame and indignity I suffered in those labor gangs, Conners," he said. "Perhaps I was tired of seeing my people oppressed, beaten, enslaved, killed at will, without recourse."

Conners shifted faintly, and the knife was thrust against him harder. He could hear the soft breathing of the man behind him now. "I can believe that," Conners said at last. "After that scene on the balcony last week."

"Perhaps a man, getting as much money as was taken from that holdup, could do a lot for his people in a town like this."

"Could he?" Something else was in Conners's mind now, bringing a frown to his brow. "It was MacLane we squeezed. Why should you need the money because of that?" The Eurasian stared at Conners without answering, the enigmatic smile tilting his lips. "Maybe you own the Crazy Moon, not MacLane," said Conners again, his voice almost a whisper. "Maybe we put the squeeze on you when we backed the Crazy Moon into the wall."

Lee shrugged. "A man makes his investments."

"Was MacLane with you on that Arapahoe Wells holdup?"

"No," Lee said, pursing his lips. "MacLane looked like he was going to be the power in Table Rock, and I thought it would be wise to align myself with him. He was glad to sell me shares in his cattle enterprises. I soon found myself with controlling interest."

"He sincerely thought Dad had rustled those cows, then?" asked Gordon.

"Yes, he did. Charlie Fontenelle and Tom Union changed the brands for me and planted them in your father's pastures."

"That does bring us to Fontenelle, doesn't it? What was he doing with that burned security?"

"It was one your father picked up," said Cheney. "I was caught in Utah without funds that year and had to pass it. Your father came across it somehow. I was afraid he would trace it to me. Apparently, Tom Union got hold of it when they hanged your father, and passed it on to Fontenelle. Fontenelle had some idea about blackmailing me."

"What was he doing working for Bayard?"

"One of the reasons Genghis Khan won so many wars was the number of spies he had in the enemy camps." Lee smiled.

Conners was frowning at the man in an effort to fit it all together. "What other investments did you make? Bayard said somebody had bought those houses on Peking Alley from the railroad. Nobody else in Chinatown had that much money. That would be quite an investment, wouldn't it? You'd lose a lot by that cave-in. Enough to really put the squeeze on when the Crazy Moon went on the rocks too."

"I will get my investments back," said Lee, tapping the money idly with a long forefinger.

"And build more houses on a mine tunnel," Conners said thinly. "I don't suppose you knew how dangerous they were."

"Nobody told me."

"That did leave you in ignorance, didn't it?" said Conners. "So much ignorance that you were putting the blame on Bayard's shoulders by heading that committee in his office the day I came. I can see the plight of your people *does* weigh heavy on your mind."

"You are in a poor position for sarcasm, Mr. Conners," said Lee. His smile was gone. "I think Chang had better take you out back now—"

"Gordon," somebody called, from outside. "Gordon?"

Conners heard the sharply indrawn breath from behind him, and saw Cheney Lee's chin lift. He knew it was Simms out there, and that this was the only help the man could give him. While their attention was still on the voice, he lunged forward. He heard the violent shuffle of feet behind, as Chang tried to follow with the knife.

Conners went into Cheney Lee. The man grappled him with surprising strength, trying to swing him back into Chang, but Conners twisted around against the desk, throwing Lee in Chang's path. The man with the knife had to throw his knife arm out wide to keep from stabbing Lee as he crashed into him.

Conners tore free and rolled backward, crashing into the lamp. It came over with a hiss of oil, and the room was plunged into darkness.

Conners threw himself back across the floor, seeking his gun. He went into churning legs.

"Cheney," called Faro, in his squeaking, frightened voice, trying to kick free.

Conners released him disgustedly. He heard the thud of feet beyond. On hands and knees, his fingers closed around the butt of his gun, still warm from his hand. At that moment, he heard the breathing ahead of him.

The silence had fallen so abruptly that he had not been aware of it. Now he knew why he could hear the breathing, and only that. It was a small, strained sound, so muted he could not be sure. He wondered if another man could have heard it. He wondered if that man could hear him. He held his breath, concentrating all his intense perceptions in one last effort to place it, and jumped.

There was a loud, harsh cry as he came up against a big, reeking body. He slashed with his gun. It struck metal with a shivering clang, numbing his hand. He grabbed the gun with his other hand and kept clubbing. He heard the clatter of the knife he had struck as it dropped onto the floor. He felt flesh and bone crunching beneath his blows, felt the big, struggling body falling backward.

It went to the floor between his legs. He kept striking till there was no movement. Then, gasping with the violence of the struggle, he groped around the wall to the door he had entered. It was closed. It had been Chang with the knife. That meant Cheney was out, and by another door. Conners felt his way further around the room, to the side wall where the lamp had stood, to the hangings at the rear wall. He tore these down, found a door behind.

It opened into a narrow, fetid passage. He moved down it in painful tension, feeling his way with his feet. He could see light ahead and moved faster. It had opened into the next building, but there was no building now, only wreckage lying at floor level, the flimsy rafters of a roof thrusting up at him, and further on, part of a wall.

He heard a clattering movement beyond. There was the faint, scraping shift of timbers, the small racket of something dropping off into the depths. He peered at the crazy pattern of smashed beams and gaping windows, trying to find movement. Then he saw it, and began to follow, waiting for a shot.

He crossed a canted wall, and stared down into the depths of the tunnel, unable to see bottom. There was a section of rickety stairway leading across the empty space to what was left of a second floor beyond, tilting crazily into the pit. Conners began crawling up these steps. From the street came the bizarre sounds of the celebration, and he could see the dragon now, still bowing and scraping before Cheney Lee's door.

Then, underneath the clamor from the street, he heard a small, scraping sound from ahead. It was more to the left this time. He changed his direction, coming to a line of rafters stripped of their shingles by the violence of the cave-in. The sound came again, barely audible, infinitely furtive. So far to the left it would be behind him the next time if it kept going that way. He understood then. Cheney knew he was here, and was stalking him.

He stopped all movement among the rafters, listening intently. For a moment there was nothing but the explosion of firecrackers and hoots of the crowd out there. Then another scraping, sliding sound. His skin began to prickle all over. He started moving in that direction, with infinite care. He came to a wall, still standing, the floor below ground level. He slipped down through a window to the floor, meaning to cross it.

Above him, the wall groaned heavily. His head jerked up to see it toppling. He threw himself back toward the window, trying to gauge where it would be as the wall came down. He judged it within inches, for as the open rectangle of that window came down about his body, with the studding and siding of the wall crashing onto the floor all about him, the top of the window frame itself clipped his hat, and the windowsill struck the floor against his heels.

He stumbled across the rubble of wall to where the floor of this building was brought up against the front of another. He climbed a porch and the ornamental facade swinging up onto the porch roof. This led to the roof that had slanted down into the wall that had fallen. Cheney Lee must have stood there to dislodge the wall and could not be much farther over. Conners jumped to the roof. It shook violently beneath him. He scrambled up the tilt to its peak. Cheney Lee stood on the other side, down by the eaves.

They saw each other at the same moment. They were so close Conners could see the little lines deepen about Cheney Lee's pinched lips as he fired the gun in his hand. Conners felt his own gun buck at the same time. The shots sounded simultaneously, but Cheney Lee's body jerked an instant before Conners's hat was swept off his head.

Cheney Lee fell backward off the eaves, crashing into the floor level before Conners realized his own slug must have reached the man first, jerking Lee up as he shot, so that Lee's slug went through Conners's hat instead of his head. Then Conners looked down at his gun, held hip-high.

Blackhorn's words came back to Conners with double irony—Cheney had been too close to raise his gun to arm's length.

Conners had fired without thought, his reflexes in tune to the fact that it would take too long to lift the gun out. How right Blackhorn had been in so many things. It brought a sadness to Conners, as he slipped his gun away. And with this feeling, other feelings came. He found himself analyzing them as he stared down at Cheney Lee. The sadness was still there. No vindication. No triumph. Only a tired sadness, a desire to get away.

Simms was coming across the wreckage to squat on his hunkers beside Conners, staring down into the hole at Cheney Lee's body.

"MacLane is clear," said Conners. "Lee was using him. Bayard is clear, too. Lee held up the Arapahoe Wells train, owned Peking Alley, hired Fontenelle. Do you think there's enough evidence to clear my uncle?"

"Plenty of evidence, plenty of witnesses."

"Can you take care of it now, Sheriff?"

Simms grinned. "Sure can. Bayard sent word to Cheyenne for the cavalry to come down Teton to keep those Chinese from doing anything about this. Where'll I find you?"

Conners gazed at him mutely, his eyes filled with a profound darkness.

"I honestly don't know," he said, and began walking

away. He paused then, but didn't turn around. "Lander, Sheriff. There's someone near Lander I've got to visit."

"But you're coming back, aren't you, Conners?"

As he walked away he muttered something so softly Simms could scarcely make it out, something addressed to the dead Blackhorn, about finally taking Wiwilla home.

A NOTE ABOUT THE AUTHOR

LES SAVAGE, JR., was an extremely gifted writer who was born in Alhambra, California, and grew up in Los Angeles. His second published story was "Bullets and Bullwhips," accepted by the prestigious Smith and Street's *Western Story*. Almost ninety more magazine stories, all set on the American frontier, followed, many of them published in Fiction House magazines such as *Frontier Stories* and *Lariat Story Magazine* where Savage became a superstar with his name on many covers. His first novel, *Treasure of the Brasada*, appeared in 1947, the first of twenty-four novels to be published in the next decade. Because of his preference for historical accuracy, Savage often ran into problems with book editors in the 1950s who were concerned about marriages between his protagonists and women of different races—a commonplace on the real frontier but not in much Western fiction in that decade. As a result of the censorship imposed on many of his works, only now have they been fully restored by returning to the author's original manuscripts. *Table Rock*, Savage's last book, was even suppressed by his agent, in part because of its depiction of Chinese on the frontier. It is now published as he wrote it.

Savage died young, at thirty-five, from complications arising from hereditary diabetes and elevated cholesterol. However, his considerable legacy lives after him, there to reach a new generation of readers. His reputation as one of the finest authors of Western and frontier fiction continues and is winning new legions of admirers, both in the United States and abroad.